THE REAL STORY OF O

A Reckless Comedy Of The Heart

KERRIE NOOR

CONTENTS

Ignore me at your own peril.

PROLOGUE

McTaggart had been a councillor for decades and spent most of it defending the councils' right to have decent offices. Known to many as "the Maggot," although no one could remember why, McTaggart liked to think of his nickname as a positive thing—because he cleared up issues, dispersed discontent, "like a maggot demolishing a bed sore."

McTaggart was still recovering from his TV interview a few weeks before. His main argument ("different budgets for different departments") had gone down like a lead balloon, and the "use it or lose it" theory only made things worse.

He had to reclaim his name, turn things around; the election was coming up, and he wanted to remain—keep his seat—at least until the mortgage was paid off.

Then he came up with an idea, an innovative pop-up idea stolen from his granddaughter Annabel.

Annabel had a thing for Barbie dolls, especially Barbie's camper van, and as McTaggart idly watched her pull a kitchen from the rear, an idea hit him, causing him to sit up like a jack-in-the-box.

"I've got it," he shouted.

Annabel, lost in the pleasure of rearranging her dolls, didn't hear, but by the time she had Barbie's tiny tea towels hung in a row, McTaggart had his pop-up library hung, drawn, and implemented on the back of a fag packet.

It covers all bases, he told himself; demolition of that damn wall of gratitude (which was a complete health and safety nightmare) and literature for the masses on a shoestring.

"We will embrace the digital age," he yelled at Isobel, his long-suffering wife, causing Annabel to pause over her miniature tea set and look up at her silly granddad.

McTaggart could not wait to impress the councillors, the town, the whole of Argyll. His pop-up idea was innovative, ahead of its time, not to mention a financial godsend.

"If it's good enough for Mattel Inc., it's good enough for Argyll," said McTaggart, and the council swallowed it whole. They loved the idea.

Soon they'll be everywhere, McTaggart told himself, *despite Ms Frasier and her motormouth objections.* All he needed was the right event, with the right audience and the right press; not only would they buy it, but his seat would be as safe as a Barbie in a camper van.

Chapter One

PUSS

Not all cats lick cream.

George looked at himself in the mirror. He brushed his white hair back, tidied his moustache, and slid a clean hanky into his pocket.

His phone pinged.

"Fancy a dram first?"

He stared at it. "Fancy a dram" was code for many things, "walking rather than driving" being one and "staying over" being the other.

He looked down at his trousers and peered underneath at his underpants. *Better change . . .* He sniffed. *And perhaps . . . a bit of Hugo Boss?*

He rustled through his drawer searching for "something different." George had a drawer full of "something different" which, when he swore he'd never see Beatrice again, he had planned to dispose of, either in a fire or a distant second-hand shop where no one knew him.

He stopped. Was he up for a tussle so soon?

Beatrice's jacket was on the back of her chair. She was excited, although if you saw her, you wouldn't know it. The only emotion Beatrice expressed was anger; anything else was hidden away, rarely seen, except the odd moment when George managed to "get it right in bed."

George was picking her up for the Aces High Club, and she had the sheets changed.

Beatrice looked at her phone like she had done just seconds before . . . no answer. *Bugger him,* she told herself.

She stared out of the window.

"Bugger you," she shouted, and the cat on the sink looked up with a *Me? What have I done?* look.

"Not you," snapped Beatrice. "Friggin' men—he could at least let me know."

Beatrice slid her hand onto Puss's chocolate-brown back as Puss pushed her spine into Beatrice's hand with a purr.

Puss had appeared the night of Amy's wedding, posed at the door like it was her home.

She had been lurking about the drive for days. No one knew where she came from, but everyone did that "isn't she cute" stroking as they passed, and Puss knew it was only a matter of time.

She was skinny, young, and always hanging around the outside tap, licking the drips, dozing under the hedges, with an eye on the door and her ear to the ground.

She was an expert of noise, jumping to attention at the sound of Sheryl's car or Helen's footsteps and lining up for her "isn't she cute" pat.

And it worked every time.

The first time Puss made her move, she was stopped by Helen with a breathless "Jesus" skid, the second by Sheryl with a "fucking hell" trip.

The third time it was fate, kismet, and Baby Bea.

It was late at night. Puss watched Sheryl ease a clinking box from the car as Beatrice wheeled herself down the drive with Baby Bea asleep on her knee and Steven, weighed down with Baby Bea's "I'm staying the night" paraphernalia, trudging behind.

Puss saw her chance; like a silent sphinx by the front door she waited. She had seen the door stick like wet sap, she knew it would need pushing, she had it timed, *like trapping a mouse.*

Sheryl wrestled with the key and went for a foot push; there was a clatter of bottles; the box almost dropped; she gripped it and went for a shoulder shove and grunt.

"Here, let me," said Beatrice.

"I've got it, Mum"—*grunt*—"bollocks . . . shit."

"Let me," said Steven, pushing forward.

"I said I've got it," snapped Sheryl with a shove of her shoulders.

The door burst open.

Beatrice, pissed off at the "I've got it" from her stroppy cow of a daughter, crashed her wheelchair into the hallway, jolting to a stop just shy of Sheryl's legs.

"Jesus, Mum!" snapped Sheryl.

Baby Bea jolted awake. She began to wail as Sheryl tried to keep her balance with a box full of wine.

"Fuck's sake," she snapped.

Steven, hearing the "Jesus" and the "fuck," pushed the door wide open, stumbling into the back of Beatrice's wheelchair; Baby Bea's paraphernalia scattered everywhere.

Sheryl swore, Beatrice cursed, and Baby Bea, starving, wailed like a banshee . . .

Puss, like the black flash of the Looney Tunes Roadrunner, zoomed in.

"The cat," shouted Beatrice.

"What cat?" said Steven, who had not been to Beatrice's house for quite some time.

Baby Bea wailed louder.

"The fucking cat in the garden," said Sheryl.

"There's a cat in the garden?" said Steven.

"Not now—he . . . *she* is in here now, probably shitting somewhere," said Beatrice. "Shhhh, baby darling."

"I told you—you shouldn't pat it," said Sheryl.

Baby Bea let out a louder wail.

"Pat it? *You* friggin' *fed* it," said Beatrice. "I said shhhh, baby . . ."

Silence . . .

Puss alighted herself onto the hall side table inches from Baby Bea, landing as soft as a ballerina; even the air wick didn't move.

Baby Bea watched, mesmerised.

Puss blinked at her.

Baby Bea cooed.

Puss whispered a soft meow.

Baby Bea, with an outstretched arm, cooed again, and Puss—the master of seduction—tilted her head into the small, round palm of Baby Bea, letting out a low rumble of purrs.

A piece of piss.

After a week of Puss skidding into doorways and staring into windows leaving muddy paws prints, a cat flap was built, bowls of dried cat food filled the corners of the kitchen, and Sheryl now arrived with scraps of chicken.

It was like she had been there for years.

Beatrice stroked Puss, her glass of whisky a few sips down.

"At least you don't have to bother," she muttered. "With men and all that nonsense." She stopped. "Although it's not really nonsense, is it?" She sighed. "It's the tits, isn't it? The absolute tits! The waking up, the coffee . . ." She scratched behind Puss's ear. "And if I play my cards right tonight, maybe . . . what do you reckon, Puss? Coffee in the morning, maybe some morning-afters?"

Puss purred.

"Though we're not going to tell him that, are we?"

Puss looked at her bowl; it was empty.

"Treat 'em mean and keep 'em keen . . ." said Beatrice.

Puss mimed a meow.

Beatrice pulled a packet of cat food from the Puss corner and gave it a shake.

Puss landed by the bowl with a soft thud.

"Yes, keep him on his toes, wanting more," muttered Beatrice, dribbling an excessive number of pellets into Puss's bowl as George pulled up in the drive.

George, a man who had many pasts in many countries, had been happily single most of his life. He had never planned to stay long in Argyll, until he met Beatrice.

For a man past seventy, he wore it well—he was trim but not skinny, more bordering on cuddly. And he had a sense of humour that expanded the range of just about anything; making him laugh was as easy as turning on a tap.

George knew he was a catch, that he could have any single woman in the WRI, but the truth was, he didn't care. George was one of those rare breeds who felt comfortable in his own skin, much to the annoyance of many women.

He was a man who liked his own company. He liked the freedom of doing what he wanted whenever he wanted. In the good old days, there were plenty of women happy with a bit on the side, free and frisky—not now. The women he met now wanted to know when and where and if lubricant was required, or as in one case, if sex was absolutely necessary.

Not Beatrice. She was as keen as he was—which was totally undetectable. Beatrice looked that sort who'd slap a penis under the tap and give it a good wash rather than a good seeing-to. But that is the intrigue of Beatrice: she had as many layers as an onion, most involving anger, until the sweet spot was tickled . . .

George thought about the past few weeks without Beatrice. It had been peaceful, like, funnily enough, his army years. Did he really want to go through all that again?

Was the sweet spot that good?

Sure, taming her added a certain spice to his day, and the gymnastics in bed with a disabled woman had added a certain artistic, creative element to lovemaking.

He had surprised himself *and* Beatrice.

But all this library stuff?

She was like a bull terrier, she just would not let go.

Chapter Two

POKER

A card shark relies on more than his hand to win the game.

Francis sighed; poker was not her game. She preferred whist nights, but as there were only the three of them, she was outvoted. There was a time when her living room was full, bulging with card players . . . not now. People were getting about in Zimmers, staying in, or worse: dying off. Not that the good old days were really good old days; Beatrice was a pain before she met George.

Back then, Francis worked in the Stables, a café busy with schoolchildren at lunchtime and young mothers in the afternoon. A café that sold chips and cheese with everything in portions that filled a dinner plate. Beatrice always came in the day after a card game, crashing past the tables and schoolchildren with her bag of two pennies from the nights' winnings. Watching Beatrice count out coppers was as painful as a leather G-string a size too tight—which, from the way George was sitting, was probably what he was wearing.

Thank god she didn't work there anymore. Thank God Beatrice had hooked up with George and thank God they were back together again. *Although they could tone it down with the sex innuendos.*

Beatrice slid her cards on the table, leant back in her chair, and sipped her dram. George seemed distracted, uncomfortable; she looked at his familiar weather-beaten face and wondered about his underwear. *Possibly the elephant. It's been ages since that has appeared.*

For ten years, their on-and-off relationship had been held together by a series of undergarments that was, thanks to a few loose-tongue posties, the talk of many.

George's underwear was part of his ensemble, part of the rich tapestry of their love life, lifting the mundane roll-on/off missionary position to delights of laughter, stripping, and, well . . . more laughter, although they both drew the line at selfies.

It all started with the codpiece—a codpiece George wore ten years ago, when they shifted from platonic spitfire friends to lovers.

The "first time" had been a bit of a fumble, accompanied by the odd "wait a minute, shift your leg" shuffles and ending in a soft moan.

George, unable to measure if that soft moan was for pleasure or "thank God it's over," was not satisfied; he prided himself on making a woman happy and couldn't leave it there. He wanted to make their first time unforgettable—not easy when you knew every move possible but no longer had the capabilities of doing half of them, especially when competing with past memories of a happy marriage, pre-wheelchair days.

George had a plan B—a prop.

He slid into the bathroom and appeared, silhouetted by the mirrored light, in *the* codpiece . . .

The same codpiece Beatrice, along with Sheryl, had seen worn over a panda suit at a wrestling match. The same codpiece used to seduce Sheryl's belly dancing teacher, Nefertiti, by her partner. And the same codpiece Nefertiti discarded when her partner became her ex.

It was a stunning piece of equipment, and minus the panda suit even more so. George had found it in the local charity shop, and could not believe his luck.

All it took was a few pelvic thrusts in time to the bathroom fan and Beatrice was laughing like she had smoked a ton of dope.

They never looked back.

Orgasms were no longer fought for but naturally evolved at the end of a George experience. And if they didn't, who cared?

A G-string slung across the room to the tune of whatever George had chosen was often enough; the laughter, the silliness.

It's a tough job, George told himself, *but someone has to do it.*

George developed new innovative ways to move a codpiece, discovering a side to him he never knew existed, and it was not long before they began to explore other undergarments, spending hours on the internet, studying sites for something different . . .

"How about this?"

"Interesting."

"Intrusive."

"Noisy."

"Bit gymnastic."

"Is that possible?"

And no matter how many times they looked, George always surprised her.

After a fight was the best. George and Beatrice fought about everything and never made up; rather, George would arrange to pick her up for the Aces High Club wearing his surprise underneath.

Soon, Beatrice began to dream of the next make-up surprise and started to instigate fights; she grew insatiable and George grew tired. After all, there are only so many ways you can dress up a penis, and he felt after ten years he had reached his limit.

George stared at his hand: a seven, a two, and—*oh god*—a five. He sighed; thanks to a frisky piece of Lycra loitering about his "bits and pieces," he couldn't concentrate, and his change was running low.

"Cat got your tongue?" said Beatrice. "Or perhaps an elephant?"

"Elephant?" Francis looked from one face to the other. "Must you always be so cryptic?"

"Cryptic is as cryptic does," said Beatrice with her favourite enigmatic look.

"Play your hand," snapped George.

Beatrice drained her glass.

George met her stare.

"I'll raise you!" he said, pushing forward a 2p.

"How 'bout I raise you," she said with a straight face.

"Oh, for Chrissake," muttered Francis.

"Raise me?" said George. "Don't make any promises you can't keep."

"I could raise the *Titanic* if given the right equipment," said Beatrice, absorbed in her cards.

"I'm out," Francis said with a toss of her cards; no one heard. She could have ripped her top off and screamed "come and get it" and no one would have heard. Beatrice and George had hit the guess-what's-underneath stage.

"I think I'll get the dips out," she muttered.

"Must you?" said Beatrice.

"What?" yelled Francis, heading to the kitchen.

"There are only three of us, why bother?" said Beatrice, pulling a face at George.

Francis moved to the doorway, catching Beatrice's look. "It may interest you to know my dips were greeted with sighs of delight at the last council meeting. Ms Frasier even wanted the recipe."

"Pfff, her," said Beatrice. "Does she talk with her mouth full?"

Francis laughed. "By the time she'd finished talking, the room had emptied apart for McTosser trapped in the corner and me packing up my empty dip dishes, and nothing was decided about the walls of gratitude."

Beatrice stiffened at the mention of the walls of gratitude and was just about to ask if there was a mention of her photographs when Francis's front door opened and shut with a slam followed by a "Cooee!"

As footsteps headed towards the sitting room, the three looked at each other.

"Shit," muttered George.

"Hide," hissed Francis.

"In a wheelchair?" snapped Beatrice.

"Is that Beatrice?" yelled Ms Frasier.

"Too late," muttered George.

Ms Frasier's head peered from the door; she plonked herself next to Beatrice.

"I haven't played cards in ages." She looked at Beatrice's hand. "What's a royal flush again?"

Chapter Three

MS FRASIER

A dip is only as good as what you dip into it.

Ms Frasier talked for Britain, the United States, Australia, and pretty much any country you could think of. She could talk an insomniac into a coma, and as she did, George's libido sunk into the sunset and Beatrice's excitement melted quicker than ice cream under a blowtorch, while Francis, giving up on her dips, began to pack up as loudly as possible.

"The game's finished," Francis said, crisply collecting cards; she slapped them into their pack. "You're too late."

"And your dips?" Ms Frasier said coquettishly.

Francis stopped. "My dips?" She flashed a look at Beatrice. "You came *here* for *my* dips?"

"Well I didn't come here for the cards, not my thing. I am more a backgammon sort of woman, not that I have any time for *that* these days, what with all the meetings."

She poked at a solitary bowl of guacamole. "Any biscuits, or is there just these crisps?" She lifted one, sniffed it, and placed it back in the bowl. "I'm more a cracker person . . . oatcakes at a push, definitely not those nacho-tortilla things."

"It is guacamole," muttered Francis, grabbing the almost-empty bowl of crisps. "What do you expect, cupcakes?"

"No one eats them," muttered Ms Frasier, "no matter how good the dip is. Sometimes foreign should just stay that—foreign . . . take snails . . . the French can keep 'em."

"You were talking about meetings?" said George.

Beatrice nudged George with a *don't ask any questions* look.

"Nothing had been decided," said Ms Frasier, "I mean nothing. I sat through a pile of talk for what?"

"They were talking, with you there?" said George.

"I mean, I love your dips, Francis, but they're hardly worth the effort of coming out. I may as well have stayed in, washed my hair, put my curlers in, and cracked open a cold one."

"Cold one," mouthed Beatrice.

"I want closure. We all want closure, something solid to hang our coats on, a decision . . . no, more than a decision—action. You're hardly going to get that from those bozos over in the community centre."

"Arrrrgh, the community centre meeting," muttered George.

"Who cares," hissed Beatrice.

"All they want to do is drink tea, eat things—even nachos—and save money. For what? That's what I say, for what? I mean when I was in Australia . . ."

Francis made a quick retreat to her kitchen. Once Ms Fraser mentioned Australia, hours would be lost, sunk into the quicksand of her reminiscing. Once she started on about "watching joeys bouncing by while sucking an *amber nectar*," folk ran for cover, or at least another room.

Beatrice's impatience began to surface.

"So, what happened at this meeting?"

"What?" said Ms Frasier.

"The meeting?" said Beatrice. "You were going to tell them I was not interested, that I was a storyteller, not some disabled mascot . . ."

"Nobody listens these days," said Ms Frasier.

"Quite," muttered Beatrice.

"Especially at meetings. For a start, no one turns their mobile off."

"There's a good reason for that," muttered Francis curtly, depositing her crisp remains in the bin.

"I mean I tried to explain about how things work and the importance of, you know, consideration, but they don't listen. Halfway through, their phones are pinging like car alarms . . . emergency this, and emergency that—half of them had left before I even got to the proposals."

"No wonder," muttered George.

"What?" said Ms Frasier.

"I said listening is a lost art," shouted George.

"You're a man after my heart," Ms Frasier cooed at George.

"Did you tell them?" snapped Beatrice.

"There was a list, of proposals to work through, and it was my job to read them out. By the time I had pulled it out . . . the list that is"—she chuckled—"the janitor had arrived, and before I had a chance to say 'amendments,' he switched on the Hoover . . . while I was still talking."

Francis appeared with a cloth and began to wipe the table like she was sanding it. Ms Frasier lifted the bowl of guacamole as Francis's cloth swooped underneath.

"Francis was still clearing up her dips. Weren't you luv?" said Ms Frasier.

Francis, continuing to polish, said nothing.

"You wantin' this?" Ms Frasier gestured with the guacamole. "I could take it home. Plenty of crackers there."

"I'll get a tub," muttered Francis.

"Which reminds me: those recipes," shouted Ms Frasier. "You couldn't possibly . . ."

"Will you leave if I give them to you?" Francis shouted from the kitchen.

Ms Frasier looked from George to Beatrice. "She's a luv, isn't she?" She stopped. ". . . did you want the dip? I never asked, how rude of me."

"You take 'em," shouted Francis. "That pair have no taste."

Ms Frasier talked of fundraising and how the community centre was skint, how she had ideas bouncing around like ping-pong balls in her head—"making one quite giddy"—and before anyone could shout "get on with it" or "I'm going home," Ms Frasier had moved on.

"No one talked about the amalgamation, though they kept that quiet, let me rattle on like a prat—they had no intention of fundraising. And I didn't know anything till it was all signed, sealed, and passed . . . well almost passed."

"What is passed?" yelled Beatrice.

"They are calling it 'moving on,' 'downsizing with technology,' 'innovative,' 'one space for all,'" said Ms Frasier.

"Are you saying they are moving the library into the community centre?" said George.

"In a fashion," said Ms Frasier.

"Well, that's not *so* bad," said George.

"I could live with that," said Beatrice.

"Are you going home now?" said Francis.

"Yes, but a pop-up library—with e-books?" said Ms Frasier. "They are going to remove the computers, change the hours to one day a week, and completely stuff up my bus shelter—*and* they are cutting the staff. The janitor's been offered a street-sweeping job."

"Lumpy?" said George. "That guy is a diamond."

"Sheryl had mentioned something," muttered Beatrice.

"I sat through a whole meeting and nothing was said. I was told via, would you believe it, email. Of course, I complained, but who listens when it comes to budgets? Especially when it's an answering machine."

She paused, looking upset.

Francis handed Ms Frasier her dip with a "here, luv."

"The only thing that can save us all now," said Ms Frasier, "is the wall of gratitude." She looked at Beatrice. "And you, of course."

"Me?" said Beatrice.

Ms Frasier smiled. "I have a plan."

Chapter Four

THE PLAN

There is more to a decent set of underpants than elastic.

That night, Beatrice, over her favourite malt whisky, waited for George to appear from the bathroom. Normally she would be wondering what he was wearing, what had caused him discomfort during the card night, but not tonight; tonight she was mulling over "the plan."

She was in bed with her hair casually scrunched and her red "catch me if you can" T-shirt, which was long enough to work as a nightie, and matching red nails painted that morning. She clinked her nails against her glass as George grunted in the bathroom.

Hours before the card game, she had been excited about their reunion—George's making-up show. Not now. Beatrice's emotions were all over the place, a mixture of nostalgia, disappointment, and a vague sense of hope, and they had nothing to do with "George's show" —not that George had clocked any of Beatrice's feelings. He was too busy sitting uncomfortably, wondering if he had jumped too soon.

Beatrice thought about *her* library; it was bad enough losing her job, but the library as well? It was her second home. For years she had righted the world, bossed, organised, and shared gossip in that place. How could anyone *do* any of that in the foyer of the community centre with a coffee machine . . . and e-books?

And where would she tell stories?

"I poured you a whisky," shouted Beatrice.

"Don't strain yourself," muttered George.

"What?" yelled Beatrice.

"I said very good."

George looked at himself in the mirror and poked at his under-pants—a colourful elephant's face with a trunk that made any pelvic thrust as humorous as a John Cleese walk.

The last time he wore them was months ago, and they were a perfect fit back then; now the waistband dug into his underbelly. He sucked in his stomach and looked side-on. *All those Yorkshire puddings and roast potatoes.*

George had spent his *incognito* time with his sister, wintering his time out from Beatrice, and his sister, unlike Beatrice, was an amazing cook, with second, third, and "you may as well finish it off" helpings.

He sighed, executing a half-hearted hip circle . . . the trunk flopped in front of him like a wet sock.

"What do you think of the plan?" yelled Beatrice at the bathroom door.

George stopped mid pelvic swing. "Plan?"

"Yes. The plan?"

George propped one leg on the side of the bath and tried a hip thrust. Did that look better?

"A plan is only as good as the executioner . . ." he yelled.

"It's not a hanging," yelled Beatrice.

George stumbled. *Shit.*

"What?" yelled Beatrice.

He grabbed the shower curtain, sending the electric toothbrush flying.

Bugger.

"I mean it's no good having a plan without proper implementa-tion," shouted George.

He scrabbled about on the floor. Why did he come back so soon? He should have waited, cut back on the Yorkshires, done a bit of walking.

"I mean I still have my petition, maybe that will help; add weight to things. What do you think? Would it make a difference?" said Beatrice.

George stood up and set the electric toothbrush back on its holder; it fired into action, spraying toothpaste everywhere, including his stomach.

Shit!

"Why don't you clean your brush, Beatrice? I've just pebble-dashed the bathroom," he shouted.

"Pebble-dashed, what's that to do with the plan? What the hell are you doing in there?"

"Implementing, Beatrice, fucking implementing," snapped George.

"Sounded like a toothbrush to me," muttered Beatrice.

"Yes, well, you should try cleaning it once in a while," said George, running a cloth over his tummy.

Beatrice shifted in her bed, her mind flitting to Ms Frasier, who seemed to know everything: the downsizing of the library equipment, the *big* book sale, and the integration with the community centre. For the first time ever, Beatrice listened to ol' motormouth Frasier.

"If it wasn't for you," said Ms Frasier, "there would be no library at all."

"Me?"

"Yes, you. You are a hero. You speak for the old," said Ms Frasier. "Every friggin' one of them."

"I'm not over the hill yet," muttered Beatrice.

"And the disabled," said Ms Frasier.

"It's just a wheelchair, I'm not a cripple. Still get about, see to my own bits and pieces, thank you, even have—god forbid it—sex, and bloody good sex at that."

George blushed a cough.

"Apparently, e-books and audio are disability-friendly," said Ms Frasier.

"There'll be a machine next," snapped Francis, "no librarian, just some sort of self-service till like in the co-op." She looked at Ms Frasier. "And a coffee machine."

"No one to talk to," muttered Ms Frasier.

"Funny enough, that is what Steven said." Beatrice sighed. "'We'll be talking to machines next,' he said. I told him he had been reading too many sci-fi books. And do you know what he said? 'There is nothing truer than sci-fi.'"

"George," muttered Beatrice, "I'm feeling a bit deflated. Why don't we just, you know . . ."

"What?" said George, crashing open the bathroom door. His plump body took Beatrice by surprise. She had heard his sister was a great cook, but . . . she eyed his round stomach.

"Maybe you should give your sister's cooking a break," she said.

"What's that supposed to mean?" snapped George.

"Just that it spoils the effect of a florescent trunk. It's sort of lost under"—she waved with her hand—"that."

"Under what?" George sucked in his breath.

"Under your stomach, what have you been eating? Pork pies for breakfast?"

"She doesn't do pork," said George, holding in his stomach. He looked at himself in the mirror. "I just sat through two hours of cards and bullshit talk in this, and for what? You to make a comment about my stomach?"

"I didn't ask you to," said Beatrice.

"Ask?" said George. "You don't ask, you expect, and this"—he attempted a pelvic swing—"is a given."

"Hmm," said Beatrice.

"What do you mean *hmm*?"

"It's just that I have a lot on my mind, and I fancied a chat rather than . . . you know . . . the usual," said Beatrice.

"You don't want the usual?" George relaxed. "Not even a twirl?"

Beatrice shook her head. "The whole world is changing."

"Bit dramatic," muttered George.

"I know, but we have to make a stand. All this change, machines . . . I mean who do *they* think *we* are? Cannon fodder, to be herded about, shoved here and there?"

"Shoving? Who's shoving who?" muttered George.

"It's our money, and they just spend it on whatever the fuck they like—regeneration? Who the fuck came up with that bullshit?"

"Integration," muttered George; he looked in the mirror again. "It's the roast. There's always seconds."

He sighed at Beatrice. "My sister cooks for an army. Comes from doing it for a living, I suppose."

Beatrice patted the bed.

He looked at her.

She patted his side again with a smile; he sat beside her.

"Just as well I'm a lousy cook then." She laughed.

Chapter Five

LUMPY

Listening moves mountains.

The event was to be held in the foyer of the community centre beside the wall of gratitude. McTaggart, embracing his "man of the people" philosophy, bypassed the admin, the publicity officer, and the finance department, nabbing Lumpy the janitor instead.

Lumpy, who was in the middle of sorting a urinal at the time, was completely unimpressed. He was up to his eyes in DYI-ing on a budget; organising a "do" was as plausible as him erecting a pole in the foyer and dancing up it.

He stared at the elegantly dressed Maggot, his hands as soft as putty—the sort of hands that would have trouble manipulating a can opener, let alone a wrench.

Not even an "are you busy?" or a "shall I come back later?" Just in and out like a wank job leaving a list a mile long.

McTaggart assumed Lumpy's silence was because he cared. He hadn't a clue about silent anger, that Lumpy was so mad he couldn't speak without swearing; forty years of marriage and an angry partner had taught him nothing. McTaggart was as oblivious to Lumpy's feelings as he was to the moods of his wife.

Lumpy had been a loyal man, a good man who loved his work in the community centre; for years he had worked his balls off for the friggin' council, and for what?

A golden handshake with a street broom?

They called it gutter hygiene—like that made a difference. It was still broom pushing, bin filling, street cleaning.

Well fuck the lot of 'em, he thought, and without a glance at the list, he screwed it into a ball and kicked it in the bin, just as Ms Frasier walked in.

"I hear there's a 'do' happening," she said.

Lumpy groaned. He'd never get that urinal fixed before tea break now.

Two days later, Sheryl and Steven arrived at Beatrice's drive to see Beatrice circling the garage with her usual impatience, George with his head in a box and Helen talking about "it" being "somewhere."

"Somewhere is the same as anywhere, nowhere and I haven't a clue where," snapped Beatrice. "And we need it *now*. Ms Frasier has it all organised."

"We're here as ordered," shouted Steven with a jokey knock on the door.

Beatrice spun her wheelchair around and spied Baby Bea in Steven's arms, and her face softened.

Baby Bea, spying Puss, stuck out her arm with a chuckle.

Puss, mid parading, looked up at her bosom buddy and stopped.

"You should have said you wanted it kept," said George, peering from a box. "I mean there's been a lot going on." He opened the box; old photographs and papers fluttered to the ground. "We're not mind readers," he muttered.

Puss gave Baby Bea a silent meow.

Baby Bea struggled to get down.

"We could make a new one," said Helen.

"No, it has to be the same. That's what Ms Frasier said," said Beatrice.

"Why?" said Helen.

"'Cause she says so."

"She?" Steven looked at his wife.

Sheryl shrugged. "I know as much as you do."

"Well it's not here," said George, shoving whatever he could back into the box.

"Bugger," snapped Beatrice. She circled her wheelchair around to spot Baby Bea attempting to wriggle out of Steven's arms. "Maybe Baby Bea knows," she cooed.

Steven slid Baby Bea to the ground; Puss moved in for a back rub.

"It'd be easy to copy," said Sheryl, "we just need more egg boxes. You're making a big deal out of nothing."

Beatrice swung her chair inches from Sheryl. "Saving our library is not nothing . . ."

"Haven't you done that?" said Steven.

Beatrice turned to Steven. "If *they* have *their* way, the library will be as personal as an airport. There'll be no chatting or waiting for the bus, just a conveyer belt, a chocolate machine full of out-of-date Twixes, and fines."

"The only person that waits for the bus is *her* . . . motormouth," said Steven.

"How can anyone think about books or storytelling when this so-called pop-up library is popped up in the corner of a foyer, the pathways of play groups, after-school clubs, and the art club's still life class?" huffed Beatrice. She reversed into a pile of boxes. One cluttered onto her shoulder; she shoved it aside.

"I mean I am as open-minded as the next, but who is going to search for a tapestry book when the drawing of bits and pieces in the next room is going on? That's enough to put you off your cross-stitch." She smiled at her own wit and made to move forward; her wheel caught on the corner of the box.

George made to help.

"I can do it," she snapped.

She pushed and huffed, unaware that Helen, behind her, slid her foot onto the cardboard and eased it out. Beatrice wheeled forward.

"And it's all on my shoulders"—she wheeled—"to protect the inno-cent, the readers, the public." Beatrice stared at her unimpressed audience. "Well, that's what she"—Beatrice glared at Steven—"ol' motormouth said."

"Mum, that is as believable as George doing a striptease," said Sheryl.

George, with an embarrassed cough, muttered about the recycling bin and headed outside.

"She did too," said Beatrice.

"Pfff, her," muttered Steven. "We used to duck behind the desk when she came into the library."

Beatrice huffed.

"The readers would race to the computer room and slide earphones on and you'd lock yourself in the kitchen."

"Aye well, that was then, not now," said Beatrice, "and you should be grateful."

"For what?"

"When she—*we* save the library and you get back all your days again."

"One day a week is fine for me," said Steven. "I get to be a dad."

"I found it," shouted George from outside.

"Where?" said Helen.

"In the recycle bin."

"Oh, forgot about that," muttered Helen with a guilty look.

"Thank God for the council cuts," shouted George. "Years ago this monstrosity would have been picked up and incinerated by now."

"My point exactly," said Beatrice. She stopped.

George appeared from the corner, clutching a crumpled pile of smudged egg boxes, looking like a paper mâché left in the rain.

He held it up like a victory medal.

A box flopped to the ground.

"Not exactly the same," muttered Helen.

Another tumbled.

"I think we got some egg boxes somewhere," said Sheryl.

Beatrice threw her daughter a caustic look. "*Somewhere* is as useless as *anywhere*, and *when was the last time you saw it?*"

Chapter Six

SUPERGLUE

The recycling of egg boxes is not always a good thing

It took a day for Helen and Sheryl to collect enough egg boxes, an afternoon for Helen and Sheryl to reproduce Beatrice's ghost pumpkin design, and an hour to get Ms Frasier drunk enough to divert her from her strategic planning.

Ms Frasier, excited that her plans were actually being taken seriously by someone other than the three-year-old next door, was around at the crack of dawn. With a whiteboard under her arm and a set of plans tucked under the other, she had woken Helen and Beatrice up and called Sheryl. By the time Sheryl had arrived, Ms Frasier had the plans spread out on the table, the whiteboard stuck on the fridge, and Beatrice and Helen listening with a great amount of eye-rolling.

"We can take 'em here and get out here," she said, leaning over an incomprehensible plan on the table. "Or here and here . . ." She stood up with a satisfied smile. "Another option."

Sheryl, Helen, and Beatrice had no idea what she was talking about.

"I think you are complicating things," said Helen. "I mean it's a car park, not a battlefield."

"But it's all in the parking," continued Ms Frasier. "You have to get it right or else . . ."

Beatrice pulled her whisky bottle from the cupboard.

"And it's not like the car park is going to be empty," said Sheryl. "You can't bank on a position—so to speak."

Ms Frasier moved from the plans to the whiteboard, pointing to a tangle of arrows.

"Which brings me to plan B," she said.

Sheryl looked at the arrows. "You mean arrive early."

"Well yes," muttered Ms Frasier.

"Won't our cover be blown?" said Helen with a side glance at Sheryl.

"Have a whisky," muttered Beatrice filling a glass. She slid it across to Ms Frasier.

Ms Frasier sipped an "arrrrh."

"Not necessarily," said Ms Frasier. "It's all in the spatial awareness" —she eyed her audience—"and of course the wind chill factor."

"Wind chill factor? We're not in Canada," laughed Sheryl.

Ms Frasier drained her glass. "There is always wind to consider," she muttered with a small belch.

"Plenty more whisky," said Beatrice . . .

Four whiskies later and the whiteboard was in the spare room, the plans tossed on the floor, and Ms Fraser in full Aussie lingo mode watching Beatrice's video on the kitchen TV.

Beatrice had tried to convince her that having "done this sort of thing before," she "had the timing perfected."

"Who needs plans when you're dealing with an expert," said Beatrice, "especially when it comes to the deconstruction of egg boxes?"

When that didn't work, Beatrice flicked on her YouTube video and was soon beginning to regret it.

Ms Frasier, it seemed, was the only person in Argyll who had not seen the video of Beatrice in the Taj, which, having been filmed by a primary school girl who had still to learn how to zoom without making an audience feel sick, required pausing with an annoying frequency. Ms Frasier was gobsmacked, talking full speed like an Australian in a comedy sketch, while Helen and Sheryl were using the video as a reference for Beatrice's costume.

"Stop there . . . no there," shouted Sheryl more than once, causing Beatrice to jump like Puss at a door slamming.

Beatrice's patience was draining quicker than a bath plughole.

"In all my years in the army, I have never seen anything like it," said Ms Frasier. "I mean the nipper"—the three-year-old next door—"described it to me, but jeez . . ."

Beatrice glared at Ms Frasier.

"I thought she was *taking the mic*," continued Ms Frasier. "Making up porkies." She grabbed Helen's arm. "They wanted to show me. 'No,' I said, 'I will watch this with *me ol' mate, me ol' cobber . . .*'"

"Must you use such fruity language?" said Beatrice, taking the whisky bottle from her.

"Stop," shouted Sheryl.

Beatrice jumped. "Jesus, what for?"

"It's the lay of the skeleton. Just need to capture it on . . . there . . ."

"That's a skeleton?" said Helen. "I thought it was a tombstone."

"It *is* a tombstone," said Beatrice through gritted teeth.

"Looks more like a penis," said Ms Frasier. "Mind you it is ages since I've seen one. Men my age are dribbling drongos; fair puts a sheila off. I mean the chances of them getting a stiffy is as likely as George fitting into a leotard."

Helen stopped mid supergluing. "How much have you had to drink?"

Beatrice, without offering any more to Ms Frasier, filled her whisky glass. "I'll have you know he's taking up jogging."

"Won't stop him dribbling," Ms Frasier muttered. She stopped. "Is that you, Bea . . . on the floor?"

Ms Frasier grabbed the remote, rewound, and replayed. "Shame about the knickers."

"Yes, well, I had no idea the whole world and his dog would see . . . must you play that again?"

"Did you get that, girls?" said Ms Frasier. "The angle?"

"Actually, we don't need *that* angle," said Sheryl.

"I think we got all we want," muttered Helen.

"This video is pure gold," said Ms Frasier. "Imagine with an accordion player—very chipper."

"Chipper?" said Helen.

"Give me that," snapped Beatrice, grabbing the remote. She

switched the video off, tossed the remote across to Sheryl, and glared at Ms Frasier.

Ms Frasier, oblivious to the glare, began reeling off the names of a few accordion players.

"Over my arse," snapped Beatrice. "It took long enough for this . . . this . . . humiliating Taj saga to die down, let alone the other video. I don't want it all dug up again. I want to be remembered for my stories, not my knickers, and you can stuff your accordion."

"There's another video?" said Ms Frasier, making a mental note to talk less and listen more.

"Kilmory," said Sheryl before catching Beatrice's "shut up" look.

"Well yes, but . . . it's confidential," muttered Helen. She turned to Sheryl. "Or something . . ."

Ms Frasier's mind whirled. "I know a few folk in Kilmory," she muttered. "I think there's an Australian there too."

"Jesus," muttered Beatrice.

"They owe me a few favours," said Ms Fraser.

"How could anyone possibly owe a drongo like you a favour," snapped Beatrice.

Ms Frasier smiled. "You'd be surprised."

Chapter Seven

THE PUMPKIN AND THE TOMBSTONE

The filming of an event is no more accurate than the telling of it —not when there is editing involved.

Sheryl reversed her van into the disabled car space of the library. Helen jumped out of the van, ran to the back, opened the door, and smiled at Beatrice.

Beatrice smiled back.

It was late afternoon and schoolchildren were filling the car park heading for the after-school club in the community centre.

At first, no one took any notice of the van.

Beatrice was feeling like a winner. Her costume was the absolute *tits*, way better than the original, despite several "are you sure" from Sheryl and Helen.

It was larger, brighter, bolder, and it took an age to reverse into the van; just perfect for stealing the show. With a mask to hide behind if, god forbid, Ms Frasier had done something stupid with the YouTube videos.

Beatrice positioned herself as Sheryl lowered the ramp, slowly revealing a Beatrice never seen before.

Children stopped.

"It's her," shouted a small girl.

"From the Taj . . ." shouted another.

Some started to cheer as Beatrice threw her best regal wave.

Helen bounded into the back of the van.

"Have you heard from George?" she said.

Beatrice shook her head.

"I think I saw him driving into the co-op," said Sheryl, trying to sound hopeful.

"The co-op? At this time?" said Beatrice. "He'll never get out in time. Just as well I have you two."

Helen threw Sheryl a look.

"Yay!" shouted a few children.

At one time, the foyer was big enough for Lochgilphead. It was an empty square space with the odd unwanted table and a large notice board which few read except to find out when the next dance class was on.

The walls of gratitude were erected in each corner to enhance the space, feed community spirit, celebrate Lochgilphead's success, and hide the damp patches. The walls expanded when needed to make one big wall for exhibitions, which was great until someone hurled several spit bombs at the entrance, and the reception area was moved into the foyer.

The reception area being a large disabled-height desk and two couches donated by the Red Cross shop, leaving little room to swing a cat, let alone expand the walls of gratitude.

McTaggart watched the foyer fill with people . . . there were more than he expected, many unknown.

The community centre staff loitered by the reception desk, along with McTaggart's best pal from the local press (who had already written the story).

Bill was sitting on the couch with a clear run to the exit. Beside him sat a few *unknowns* looking like they were out for a good time, and on the opposite couch sat the job centre girls.

For a flashing moment, McTaggart doubted himself . . .

Did he have enough wine? Cheese?

Lumpy appeared with a sniff, thumped a pot of hot tea down on the table, and went back to the kitchen.

"Thank you, Lumpy," said McTaggart.

"Go fuck yourself," shouted Lumpy from the kitchen.

McTaggart, a little perturbed, threw a *see what the janitor's up to* look at Isobel.

Isobel, with a stoical slump, went to investigate.

McTaggart looked into a sea of faces searching for a friendly face and smiled at his boss.

"We are looking at a new dawn, a new age of technology . . ." he started.

The reporter nodded and smiled at him.

" . . . and it's up to all of us in Argyll to embrace the change," said McTaggart.

"Thought you said there'd be wine," muttered a small voice from the couch.

"Yeah, and where's the cheese?"

With a dramatic skid, Ms Frasier pulled up beside Sheryl's van, screeched to a halt, and jumped out of her car.

"You ready?" she shouted, peering into the back of the van.

What she saw took her breath away . . .

A giant orange pumpkin with an even larger tombstone at its back and Beatrice's feet poised on the bottom ledge of the wheelchair in black shoes and stocking socks.

"Can you drive in that?" said Ms Frasier.

"Of course, what do you take me for?" said Beatrice. "Sheryl, lower the plank."

"It's lowered," yelled Sheryl.

"Oh, bit hard to see in this angle," muttered Beatrice.

"Did you do a test run?" said Ms Frasier.

"We did try to tell her," said Sheryl.

"But would she listen?" added Helen.

"When it comes to test runs, you can't have enough," huffed Ms

Frasier, launching into a speech about the army's policy on the importance of such things until Beatrice told her to shut up.

The car park was now full of children, mothers, and the odd library visitor, including Cora and Sky—the two sisters who had videoed Beatrice at the Taj—and their mother Janice.

Janice, with a long "not again" face, watched on as the wind began to pick up.

Cora and Sky skipped about, excited.

Beatrice's green egg boxes rattled with each move; they were piled so high they caught on the van roof as she approached the ramp.

Beatrice attempted a repositioning reverse.

Ms Frasier huffed into the wind.

"She's coming out!" shouted a wee one.

"Yay!" shouted a few.

"Don't you dare film this," snapped Janice to her daughters.

"Everyone else is," said Sky, ignoring her mother.

Beatrice looked out on the children's faces as the wind blew an egg box into her face.

"This is going to be epic," she yelled a little manically for Sheryl's liking.

"I'd feel better if George were here," Sheryl muttered to Helen.

"Don't worry," yelled Ms Frasier into the wind, "I've pushed a few wheelchairs in my time. And I am a master of emergency."

Sheryl threw a *typical* look at Helen.

The ramp stopped, started, and juddered to a halt inches from the ground.

"Ready," said Ms Frasier.

"For anything," shouted Beatrice.

"Yay!" shouted the children.

As Sheryl texted George.

McTaggart was in full flight; it seemed like everyone was listening.

"All this will be gone," he said with a sweeping gesture toward the walls of gratitude.

The audience stared at the foyer the size of a post office.

"Even my desk?" yelled the receptionist.

"I thought those gratitude walls were fixed, permanent-like," said a voice from the back.

"Nothing is fixed." McTaggart smiled. "We are looking at a new dawn, a new age . . ."

"My desk is fixed," yelled the receptionist.

"Where will I hang the town's artwork?" shouted McFlaherty, the art teacher, who was standing behind the couch.

"Perhaps this"—McTaggart made another sweeping gesture—"is not the place for art shows, bodies . . . and . . . well, desks."

"Not the place?" snapped McFlaherty. "There's nowhere else."

"And where's the signing-in book gonna be? In the gents'?" yelled the receptionist.

"My son hung his first painting in here," said the young woman squashed next to McFlaherty.

"Aye, so did the wife, nobody else would have it," yelled the voice from the back.

A few chuckled.

"We at the council are all about changes, improvements," said McTaggart, "working together for a better Argyll."

"Better offices," mumbled McFlaherty.

"Making the most of things," said McTaggart. "That is our motto."

"Most of things?" shouted the voice from the back. "Since when did the council make the most of things for us? You've just done up the headquarters—new carpet."

"Aye—shagpile," shouted his pal.

"We do not endorse shagpile," sniffed McTaggart. He turned to the kitchen. *Where is that wine and the nibbles?*

"We don't have carpet," muttered the woman on the couch. "We have a few hessian sacks and leftover tiles. Try living with that in this so-called global warming."

"We're not here to talk about global warming," said McTaggart.

He looked around. *Where did all this rabble come from?*

The reporter, smiling, pulled out his notepad.

"Global warming my backside—my house is four walls of damp. It's like living in an icebox," said the voice from the back.

"Aye, so's mine," muttered his pal.

"So cold my feet stick to the tiles. Got a food parcel from the council. Try cooking that on a one-ring stove with two plastic *Flora* cartons . . ."

"We're are not here to talk about food parcels," said McTaggart. "That's the social work."

"Social work? Their idea of a food parcel is pasta with no sauce, a packet of soya mince, and tub of jam. My wean doesn't even like jam, she likes Wotsits, hummus, and olives," said the voice from the back.

"Olives my arse, what wean likes olives? You're taking the piss," said his pal.

"Piss? I'll tell you what piss is, this here tea. Where's the fucking merlot?" said the tiny woman at the front.

"Aye!" yelled the receptionist.

McTaggart caught sight of Bill looking at his watch.

"Lumpy!" shouted McTaggart, "where's *that* wine?"

Chapter Eight

THE MOB

One plan often has more than one interpretation.

Ms Frasier pondered part two of her plan, which up to now had been in the development stages.

Ms Frasier told Mr McTaggart that she would do the publicity, let folk know about the "do" in the community centre.

Mr McTaggart told her not to bother, that the invitations had been sent, and assumed when Ms Frasier said nothing, she was doing nothing. After all, she hated the idea and had argued for Britain about it. He had no idea she had a plan. That she had lain awake at night with her precise army mind working overtime, plotting and planning, or that she had the powerhouse of Beatrice backing her every inch.

He thought she'd go home to moan, text, talk, drink tea or whatever the hell she drank—not make posters and leaflets, tell the world.

She didn't speak for several minutes . . .

I need a crowd, a rabble, a mob, thought Ms Frasier. She sipped her empty glass.

Helen and Sheryl looked at each other.

A silent Ms Frasier was unheard of . . .

"If that McTaggart wants an audience," she finally said, "I'll give him one."

"Give him one?" said Beatrice.

Puss, poised by her bowl, meowed.

"I need a throng," muttered Ms Frasier.

"A G string?" said Helen.

"A mob," said Ms Frasier.

"Oh a mob?" said Beatrice.

"Yes. Where can I get one?"

The three women stared, superglue poised, as Ms Frasier, without waiting for an answer, grabbed her jacket, and muttering about Mohammedan moving mountains, headed for the job centre.

The three women watched her head off.

"Mob?" said Beatrice. "What does she need one of them for?"

She stopped . . .

That woman could bully the Pope into a striptease. Getting hold of the surveillance videos in Kilmory would have been as easy as pulling open a packet of crisps.

"Oh god, the video."

Ms Frasier planted leaflets and posters in the job centre advertising free booze and all the cheese you can eat.

Mr McTaggart wants *you*—
Yes, *You*!
Come along,
Listen to his plans for the new digital age,
And speak to a Councillor that listens.

The two receptionists/admins/benefits experts/agony aunts stared at the leaflets.

"Isn't he the Maggot?" said one.

"Who cares?" said the other. "There's free wine. We could get a few in before the pub."

Beatrice, a few whiskies down, began to mull over Ms Frasier's quest for a "mob."

Ms Frasier had really annoyed her, and she was determined to make Ms Frasier eat her words *and more*.

She drained her glass.

"If there is going to be a mob, then we need to aim bigger," said Beatrice.

Sheryl and Helen, supergluing like mad, looked up.

"Bigger?" muttered Sheryl.

"Yes, bigger—huge," said Beatrice.

"Huge?" Helen stopped.

"Actually," said Beatrice, topping up her dram, "massive."

"But we have only today," said Sheryl.

"And the drying time has to be calculated in," muttered Helen.

"Drying time? A mere technicality," said Beatrice.

"Hardly mere," muttered Helen.

"We are saving our community," said Beatrice.

"Saving?" Sheryl looked at Helen.

"Yes, saving, and we must think larger than life itself," said Beatrice with drama.

"Mum, I think you've overdone the whisky."

Beatrice didn't hear. In her head was a picture of what she wanted . . . and she could not rest until it was done.

By the time they were finished, it was dark outside, the kitchen was astray with bits of egg boxes, empty mugs, and glasses, and Puss was by her empty food bowl meowing like her throat had been cut.

Beatrice had made several phone calls and sent Sheryl on several trips for "as many egg boxes as you can fit in that car of yours," and Sheryl was quite frankly knackered.

She stared at the finished product. *It's sort of a cross between a tombstone and . . .* She looked at Helen. "Does that look like a tombstone to you?"

"It depends which way the wind blows," muttered Helen.

Sheryl and Helen had suggested a "test run," but Beatrice, with a dismissive wave, shouted, "You're talking to an expert. We've done it before—haven't we, Sheryl?"

Sheryl didn't argue; she didn't see the point. Her mum had reached the stage of whisky-drinking where fantasy, illusion, and ego collided. Her mum was oblivious to reason, and she wanted to go home.

"If they thought I was something on YouTube . . . well, just wait, and you two"—Beatrice gestured with her glass—"will be remembered, your names engraved . . . put on plaques . . . you'll be friggin' heroes."

At which point Sheryl removed the whisky bottle and fed the cat.

On the day of the "do," McTaggart arrived early as is his usual, expecting a bit of banter with those who worked in the community centre.

The foyer was decorated for a birthday party scheduled later that evening. It was littered with *seventy years young* helium balloons and streamers of all colours, and the wall of gratitude, which McTaggart presumed was to do with the birthday, was covered up with sheets.

A smarter man might have peeked, but not McTaggart; he was too excited. Soon his pal in the press would be here listening to *his* clever idea, along with Bill, his line manager, a man with a strong "the community of the people for the people" ethos. He was youngish and idealistic and had a list a mile long to work through.

McTaggart searched for Lumpy, and when he couldn't find him, he set up the table, and by the time McTaggart had found the biscuit box, the first of the public had arrived, along with Isobel, McTaggart's wife, and a sulky Lumpy.

Clutching his mug of Nescafé, McTaggart mentally reviewed his speech as the foyer began to fill with people, some curious, others for the free booze. Disappointedly, they stared at the plate of empire biscuits and jug of milk. "Not even a cheap merlot," muttered one of the women from the job centre.

"Typical," muttered the other.

"Lumpy," shouted McTaggart, "where's the wine?"

Chapter Nine

STAR WARS AND MORE

A rissole, a rissole, my kingdom for a rissole!

The schoolchildren skipped around the car park, wondering what their storyteller was going to do, until the childcare assistant appeared at the community centre's entrance.

"She's here," shouted one of the boys.

"She'll be telling stories soon," yelled another.

"Shhh, there's a meeting. And you must be . . ." The assistant, catching sight of Beatrice steering herself out of the van, stopped.

The fluorescent-green tombstone on the back of Beatrice's wheelchair wobbled, despite Helen's best attempts to secure the egg boxes. It was so high that the slightest bump had it ricocheting like a tower of bricks in a wheelbarrow.

Sheryl, under the instructions of Beatrice via scribbled diagrams, had constructed an orange and green pumpkin around Beatrice; her face was hidden behind a pumpkin stem. Helen called it "a miracle of deconstructed egg boxes"; Beatrice called it her "bright idea."

It was an epic outfit, with a scary face on the pumpkin stem and another on the black cape swinging about the tombstone and "rest in peace, pop-up library" written underneath.

And the best bit: a trap door in the tombstone with the petition behind it, which both Beatrice and Sheryl claimed was their idea.

It was a costume that silenced many and stopped cars.

"Jesus," muttered the assistant.

"What was that?" said a wee girl.

"Nothing . . ." said the assistant.

The apparition inched forward slower than a sloth on Valium.

A car passing by tooted.

"That's the storyteller," said a stout boy.

The assistant ushered him inside with a "Shhh."

The stout boy stopped. "It is, I heard her speak. *She's* the storyteller."

"Quickly," hissed the assistant, and as the last child filed in, she stopped, caught sight of the dreaded Ms Frasier, and her heart went out to McTaggart, a man who no one usually felt sorry for.

George was hiding in the co-op, swithering whether to join Beatrice or not.

He had been given orders and sent garbled texts, most of which had him seriously wondering about heading back to his sister's—indefinitely.

In fact, if it wasn't for his sister's "not today, I'm busy," he might have been heading up to Oban just now . . .

It was like the petition all over again.

He paused in the vegetable aisle. *Do I want to go through all that again?*

When George stomped away from Beatrice's petition fiasco, he disappeared from all; it took a week for him to calm down, arriving at his sister's with not a word of where he'd been.

"That Beatrice is a hill best left for goats to climb," he said, dumping his bag in the spare room. "I am never seeing her again."

Which he continued to say at least once a day, along with "she'd drive a man to drink."

"But you like your drink," tutted Morag (her usual answer).

Morag believed her brother as much as she believed Trump's claim that global warming didn't exist; within a day, George was bored, flicking his way through daytime TV.

When Morag and George first met Beatrice, they hated her on sight and couldn't understand how such a nice man as Robert could hook up with her. Over the years, they watched Robert put up with Beatrice's antics—antics that would turn a saint to sin—and neither understood why, until Robert died.

Beatrice joined the Aces High Club when Robert died, soon beating everyone including George. Watching *her* play cards did something to George; each time she won, his arousal expanded like a hot air balloon.

George started to stay, hang around; a single Beatrice kept him interested. He stopped flitting in and out of Argyll and began to visit his sister more, cheering up her lonely afternoons. It was nice having him about, and Morag's hatred of Beatrice mellowed to a "better the devil you know" bordering on silent gratitude.

When George and Beatrice first became an item, Morag gave it a week; in fact, it took a month for the couple to argue.

Soon it became a pattern: George would arrive, stay a night or two —just long enough for the two of them not to annoy each other. Then they would fall out and George would appear at Morag's where she would cook for him and over a dram half listen to his story.

The George-and-Beatrice saga added something to Morag's chats on the phone and coffee mornings. All her pals loved to hear about "the pair"; some even suggested she "write a book about it."

And the best thing about Beatrice by far was her ability to "roll with the punches."

"I can shout till my throat's dry and she wouldn't bother," said Morag. "Insults roll off her like a ball on a snooker table, and she never expects an apology, she just acts like nothing has happened."

George stared at the row of half-priced courgettes, Beatrice's favourite vegetable and one she liked to buy with a coquettish look just for him . . .

"And how many people get to wear Lycra at our age?" said his sister (more to herself). "Can't think of anyone who'd like to see me in it, even for a laugh."

He fingered a courgette and plopped one in a bag. He could hear people talking of an apparition in the community centre car park.

"She's heading for the community centre," said one. "Although at the rate she's going it will take her a week."

"Should have done a test run," muttered another, "always do a test run with these things."

George smiled to himself; he could just imagine Beatrice, determinedly pressing on.

He slid several more courgettes into a bag, moved to the alcohol section, and stared at the malt whiskies.

She'll be wanting to celebrate, he told himself with a small smile. *Or a shoulder to cry on . . .*

Isobel was in the kitchen pouring wine into an "I luv Argyll" mug.

The kitchen, like every other room in the community centre, was set off from the foyer, and right by the door of the kitchen was Isobel's husband, pontificating to all in front of him. She had a "braw" view of his back, which many considered the best view.

Isobel leaned against the bench, watching Lumpy sip and talk at the same time.

On the table in the corner was a large cake with "seventy years young" scrawled across it, along with a display of food that only a daughter in love with her Star Wars fan dad (first three movies only) could provide.

Across the top of the cake lay Princess Leia seductively holding the seventies-style "seventy," her tongue licking the Y with delight. Standing on guard at the bottom were stormtrooper cupcakes and marshmallow Ewoks. By the side was a huge sausage roll in the shape of the giant wormlike creature Jabba, surrounded by tiny R2-D2-shaped sausages standing at attention: an impressive feat, especially viewed by someone who struggled to make a rissole.

For several minutes, Isobel stared at the display as Lumpy topped up his drink.

Lumpy was not a wine drinker—more a beer man—but as the only other choice was co-op bargain teabags and out-of-date lumpy Nescafé, wine seemed the better option. Besides, he had earned it.

Lumpy talked of his job and how much he loved it and how he had planned to keep it until he retired. Isobel, with one eye on Jabba's erect sausages and an ear to her husband's speech, pretended to listen. She was an expert at half hearing while picking her nails, cleaning, or making rissoles that fell apart—*multitasking* was her middle name.

Lumpy seemed agitated, angry, and as she watched him knock back his wine like water, she wondered if she should call his woman *Mavis*.

"I know everyone who comes in," he said. "You don't need no security camera with me around. See that cake there?" He gestured with his glass. "Safe as houses, not a crumb touched before the birthday boy."

"Well that's a relief," muttered Isobel.

"I keep things safe, simple—not that that twat would notice."

Isobel looked at her husband expanding on about the joy of e-books and sighed.

"He doesn't even read e-books," she said. "The only thing he reads is the *Sun*—the *Record* at a push, though he'd never admit to it, reads it in his shed, thinks I don't know."

Lumpy pulled another "I luv Argyll" mug from the cupboard. "Why don't you join me, care of the council."

She was about to argue, make tea, and stopped . . . her husband was working through his *win 'em over* speech.

"If you think Argyll is the place for innovation," said McTaggart, "then I'm your man."

"Why not," she said. "And while we're at it, let's get out the cheese. That Jabba is making me hungry."

Chapter Ten

ENTER THE PUMPKIN

May your Ewoks be plenty.

eatrice was used to treating her wheelchair like a racing car. But, as she tried to steer it under a mask of deconstructed egg boxes flapping against a wind that could hurl a yacht across Loch Fyne, Beatrice's ability to race was as possible as a comatose turtle's.

Ms Frasier marched on, turned back, stood beside her comrade, *huffed*, marched on, turned back, and stopped . . .

"By the time we get there, the pop-up library will have popped up, closed down, and popped up again," she snapped.

"You wanted it large," came Beatrice's voice, muffled under the mask.

"There's large and then there is large," muttered Ms Frasier.

"And look, people are staring," said Beatrice into her mask. "An audience."

"No wonder—you look like you have a great big penis on your back," said Ms Frasier.

Beatrice lifted her mask. "Penis? What sort of men have you been with?"

"It's a pumpkin tombstone!" yelled the little girl heading into the car park.

Beatrice retrieved her mask.

The little girl took a picture.

"Why didn't you do a trial run, time things? In the army we always time things—down to the last second," said Ms Frasier.

Beatrice huffed behind her mask. "And that would explain the state of the world then."

She raised her mask. "I'm doing my best here to save that goddamn library and all you can do is praise warmongers."

Ms Frasier pulled the mask back in place. "We save lives in the army too, you know. When I was in Australia . . ."

"Shall I run ahead?" said Helen.

"Me too," said Sheryl.

"I'll wait with you," said a little girl.

She gazed up at her hero and caught sight of Beatrice's eye through a small hole in a free-range egg box.

"I like this costume better," she said with a soft pat on Beatrice's head and took another picture.

"Annabel" shouted a young mother, from a car.

The little girl looked up.

"Anna . . ." The mother stopped, catching sight of Beatrice. "Isn't Halloween over?"

"She's saving the library, Mummy," said Annabel.

The mother blushed. "Don't let your granddad hear you say that."

"Granddad?" Ms Frasier looked at Annabel.

"Yes, McTaggart. He should be finished soon—we've come to pick him up," said Annabel's mother.

Ms Frasier looked at her watch. "But what about the wine, the cheese?"

"Oh, that? Lumpy made a cock-up," said the Annabel's mother. "Apparently it's all but done and dusted."

"Done and dusted," snapped Ms Frasier. She turned to Beatrice. "We've got to get a move on, shake a leg."

"Shake a leg?" came Beatrice's voice, muffled through her mask.

Ms Frasier stopped, her mind whirling. Beatrice was going to take ages . . . warming up the audience was their only hope.

"I'll go ahead," shouted Ms Frasier. "Head them off at the pass; only stalling can save us now."

"Stalling?" mumbled Beatrice.

By the time Sheryl and Helen entered the community centre, Lumpy and Isobel had emptied a bottle of wine, and by the time they had made their way down the passage past the gents, Isobel had eaten several miniature Babybel Edam balls and opened another wine, and the two were toasting Jabba's glistening army of sausages.

McTaggart, who, due to the lack of Lumpy hospitality, had cut short his technology-embracing talk, was now playing a five-minute video on the flat-screen above the reception desk.

The screen usually played the same "Welcome to Argyll" video played in Kilmory reception. However, today it was playing "Pop-Up Sensations: A Look into the Future," a video made on a budget that would struggle to buy a fish supper.

The audience, subdued, bored, and wishing they were somewhere else, began to make leaving noises as the reporter, looking at his watch, put away his camera.

Sheryl and Helen caught sight of Lumpy through the kitchen door window and decided to inspect. Lumpy was a man you wanted on your side, especially when it came to causing chaos in the community centre; besides, it looked like he had a drink in his hand.

Helen and Sheryl, entering the kitchen, spied the empty Babybel wrappers, the wine bottle, and Isobel in mid conversation about her husband's rubbish choice in reading materials . . .

"'It's true, I saw it in the *Record*,' he said . . ." She laughed.

Anyone who reads the *Record* like the Bible is a tit," said Lumpy. He turned, caught sight of Helen and Sheryl, and smiled.

"My early retirement 'piss-up,' fancy joining us?"

Lumpy poured the wine; Sheryl raised her glass, spied a Babybel, and was just about to prise the wax ball open when she heard Ms Frasier . . .

"McTaggart," yelled Ms Frasier over the video, "I hear you're a man of the people."

The crowd stopped, turned to see Ms Frasier filling the entrance with her best army stance, and gasped a silent *shit!*

Ms Frasier inhaled the boredom in the room and pulled out her best weapon *ever*: cryptic words followed by . . . silence.

McTaggart fixed his gaze on motormouth Frasier.

She stared back.

"Ms Frasier, glad to see you," he said. "But we're nearly finished here."

"Are you?" she said with her best enigmatic look.

The credits came up on the video; the screen went blank.

"Yes . . ." he said.

"Well, maybe you're finished and maybe you ain't," she said.

The audience looked from Ms Frasier to McTaggart.

"Has she been drinking?" muttered the voice at the back; his pal shrugged.

"What is that supposed to mean?" said McTaggart.

"Mean? Mean! Mean is what you make it," she said.

"Definitely been on the piss," muttered the voice from the back. "She never waits for an answer."

"If you came to cause trouble, then forget it—these good people know what they want."

A few looked at each other with a "do we?"

McTaggart stared back. "Well?"

Silence.

"Nothing to say?"

Silence.

"Cat got your tongue?"

McTaggart shifted uncomfortably. *Speak . . .*

She held his gaze without a blink.

McTaggart blushed. *Get it over with . . . put us out of our misery . . .*

Silence . . .

The audience shifted uncomfortably, baffled by Ms Frasier's silence. She was never silent; words flowed from her like sewage from a broken sewage pipe. She could hold up a queue for hours with her Australia stories. No one had ever seen her silent, not even the dentist or the doctor . . .

Ms Frasier could mumble her way through a root canal treatment and talk through a pelvic examination, which was probably the reason she never married. A blow job with her talking was like trying to eat chocolate with an abscess: just not worth the effort.

Speak! Spit it out! I can't stand it!!! Thought most in the room.

They waited . . .

A car tooted, followed by another, as the children in the next room began to sing . . .

One two three four five.

Still Ms Frasier remained silent, her steely glare daring anyone to speak.

Some looked away, stared into their hands; it was as unnerving as being caught on the loo.

"Jesus," whispered one of the job centre girls. "Glad she never came to us for a benefits check."

The sound of small feet racing down a corridor filled the hall. A few looked about; Ms Frasier, however, didn't falter. *Wait,* she told herself, *Beatrice can't be long now.*

Annabel burst into the foyer. "The storyteller's coming."

"She's going to blow this meeting to smithereens."

"The storyteller?" yelled a child from next door.

"Yay!" yelled a few.

"Annabel!" shouted her Mum, passing the gents. "Annabel!" She entered the foyer. "I thought I told you to wait . . ."

She stopped, staring at the silent room and her father's grim face.

" . . . for me . . ."

At first, Annabel's mother tried to stop her daughter from yelling yet again, but when she saw her father's red face, something inside her snapped. Annabel was a free spirit, like she used to be.

McTaggart's face reddened; he glared at his daughter as Annabel filled her lungs and yelled.

"Let's help the storyteller!"

Helen, admiring the Star Wars display, absentmindedly slid a Babybel into her mouth along with a cracker, then sipped her wine.

The children in the other room could be heard singing . . .

Sheryl sang along: "*Then I let him go again . . .*"

Helen joined in: "*Why did you let him go?*"

"Wait a minute," said Isobel, "he's not talking."

"Who?" said Helen and Sheryl in unison.

"The hubby?"

"Maybe he's reading the *Record*." Lumpy laughed.

"Shhhh," said Isobel.

"Shit, neither is Herself—motormouth," muttered Helen.

They heard a car toot, followed by another, then Annabel.

"Smithereens? Storyteller?" said Lumpy. "What's going on?"

Helen looked at Sheryl. "It's about to kick off."

Chapter Eleven

THE ENTRANCE

There were two captains trying to steer that ship, and neither knew what they were doing . . .

A whirl of a wheelchair filled the silence in the foyer, followed by a muffled "move—get out the road."

Ms Frasier faltered, shifting to the side.

McTaggart saw the falter and, grabbing his chance to "wrap things up," jumped in.

"So, as you can see, a pop-up library ticks many boxes . . ."

Squeeeeeek!

McTaggart stopped.

Beatrice appeared, filling the doorway like a giant fluorescent pumpkin, her dark cloak catching on a wheel.

The reporter dropped his pad.

"Jesus," muttered McFlaherty.

The reporter scrabbled for his camera, his phone. *Which to use first?*

"Shit," muttered McTaggart.

"This is better than cheese," muttered one of the job centre girls to the other.

❄

George, spying Sheryl's van in the car park, pulled in. The car park was full, the van empty.

"Shit!" He reversed out . . . and headed down the road, finding a space a block away.

George slid his car into a space, jumped out, and began to run. Soon he was cursing his pot belly. If only it had been a month from now, after a month of jogging and Beatrice's rubbish food, he'd be able to take this block in minutes . . . as it was, he had to stop, catch his breath, and remove his jacket.

Bill stared at the apparition in a wheelchair and, unlike all the rest in the room, his face lit up . . .

He saw hope.

Bill had a disabled mother who he loved more than his precious BMW. A woman who struggled every day to shift from her bed, to the commode, to a chair, to the commode, to her bed. A woman the same age as Beatrice, hoisted, catheterised, and broken, who had given up, turned her head to the wall, and refused to watch TV, even her beloved *Strictly Come Dancing*.

Finally, he thought, *a person in a wheelchair doing something more than holding up a queue in the post office.*

Sandy, the daughter of the seventy-year-old birthday boy, had planned to arrive early. She had been reassured by Lumpy that she could come any time to sort things and that he was happy to help.

Sandy was stressed out of her box.

She had a list a mile long and a husband who had started cele-brating—in front of Sky sports.

"I'll walk," he said, flicking open his second can of beer.

Sandy, with a "whatever," lifted a box of presents, jumped into her car, and headed to the community centre, her mind whirling with what to do.

She had a box of presents artfully arranged around the Star Wars table, a sister claiming to keep Dad busy, and a dad texting, "You can't pull the wool over my eyes."

Frank, Sandy's father, was a stickler for punctuality and liked to "get there in plenty of time." Sandy had spent her childhood bored senseless in waiting rooms thanks to her father's instance of getting there an hour early.

Sandy had given him a false starting time, which was, as her husband claimed, a pointless exercise. Sandy's false times stopped working after the first "do" when he arrived to find the party in full swing.

How long could her sister keep the ol' boy occupied?

She pulled into the full car park and, like George, swore, reversed, and drove out again, searching for a space nearby, finally stopping, as George did, a block away.

She pulled a box from the car and began to run, catching up with George as he stopped to remove his jacket.

"Here, let me," panted George, gesturing to her box.

She looked at his red face and shook her head. "I've got it."

He began to cough.

She stopped. "You okay?"

When the children heard Annabel, they saw their chance. Filled with pent-up energy that only a rainy day in school can give, they jumped up from their floor mats and ran to the door.

The assistant didn't have much hope of control—she knew it, they knew it—and did she care? She had been left to run things by herself. A job way past her one-day health and safety training or meagre lower-than-a-coffee-table pay.

She gave up as quick as a click of a finger. Sliding a peppa pig biscuit between her lips, she idly texted a "come quick" to her boss, then crossed her arms and watched as the stout boy burst open the door and the others followed.

Like a rabble of Celtic warriors, they rampaged forth.

"Yaaaaaaaay!"

Beatrice, behind her mask, watched as a tsunami of children poured into the foyer, flooding the tiny space, already full to capacity. She stared up at the helium balloons nestled in the corners of the ceiling.

There were seventy, all with streamers trailing inches from the children.

The stout boy stretched to touch, possibly grab.

"Leave it," shouted McTaggart to the stout boy.

The stout boy's puffy hands twitched.

"It's for the party later," said McTaggart.

"Party?" muttered the stout boy, his hand millimetres from a streamer.

"Party?" muttered the voice from the back.

"You mustn't touch it, dear . . ." said Ms Frasier.

Beatrice rolled her eyes under her mask; even she knew that was the worst thing to say to a child, especially one who thought "no" was meant for other children.

"I'm Sandy," said Sandy, "like in *Grease*."

"Grease?" said George.

"Yes, only mum calls me Sandra."

"I see," said George.

"Well, except for Dad."

"I see," puffed George. "Can we stop for a minute?"

"He calls me princess."

"You go on, I just need to get my breath," muttered George.

"For Princess Leia."

George stopped. "I'm sorry, I can't talk and march at the same time. What did you say?"

"Leia as in *Star Wars*?" said Sandra.

"Oh, that," said George.

Sandy looked at George, his face red as he tried to catch his breath.

"You okay?" said Sandy. "Sorry I prattle on when I'm nervous. I've got this party at the community centre."

"Community centre?" said George. "That's where I am heading."

Ms Frasier didn't count on the spacing of things, always her downfall; even parking took her an age to master. It was her spatial awareness that did it: hers was fucked.

The idea was for Beatrice to circle the foyer while she surprised everyone with an unveiling on par with the Oscars. She, thanks to her many contacts, had it all set up on a remote. At one flick of a button, the sheets would drop from the walls of gratitude, the walls would unfold, and the video, along with a brass band fanfare tune, would start, revealing the show of the century.

Ms Frasier had a show that would sink McTaggart's pop-up faster than a sack of spuds in the Clyde.

She was a genius when it came to surprises, but even she, with all her army training, was not prepared for the children.

Chapter Twelve

HELIUM BALLOONS

Life is too short to waste trying to reform an arsehole.

ogether, George and Sandy talked as they walked/marched/sauntered their way to the community centre, George with his breath firmly "caught" and his face returning to its proper colour and Sandy clutching her box. She had expectations of a half-empty foyer full of bored people, a kitchen under Lumpy's control, and a bit of wine left over from the council "do."

George had no expectations apart from Beatrice's egg box creation not standing the rigours of an all-out "sit-in" or whatever Ms Frasier called it.

Neither had any idea of what they were about to walk into . . .

As they approached the car park, they stopped; they could hear children yelling and a squeaky "stop that," followed by laughter.

George and Sandy looked at each other, each thinking the other knew what was going on. When they realised neither did, they began to walk faster, working up to a sprint . . .

The two girls from the job centre ran past, giggling; a few more from the audience staggered out, followed by McFlaherty. He stopped . . .

"I wouldn't go in there."

"Why?" said Sandy.

"Bedlam," muttered McFlaherty.

They arrived at the entrance as more of the audience were leaving . . .

Nothing could have prepared them for what they saw, and if both were honest, it was better than any TV.

"Shit, the children," muttered Sheryl.

"You've a thing against children?" said Lumpy.

"No," said Sheryl, "it's Mum . . . they're like opium to her."

"Addicted," muttered Helen.

"She goes all . . . funny," said Sheryl.

"And she'll be impossible to get home," said Helen.

Sheryl opened the kitchen door to see children charging into the foyer and a panic-stricken Ms Frasier dive for the remote on the reception desk.

Using all her army training, Ms Frasier hurled herself onto the desk and grabbed the remote as a sea of children knocked her off her footing.

"Yaaaaaaaay!"

She went down clutching the remote against her chest, activating the play button . . .

"Yaaaaaaaay!"

"Jesus," muttered Helen.

Lumpy, ignoring Sheryl's "better help," wrenched her inside and slammed the door shut.

"But Mum's a genius with kids," said Sheryl, "one look from her and they'd be sorted. All we need to do is remove the mask."

"If that lot see this lot"—he gestured to the Star Wars table—"who knows what will happen."

"Jabba wouldn't stand a chance," muttered Isobel, topping up her glass.

A helium balloon exploded.

"Poor Mum," muttered Sheryl, making for the door again.

Lumpy held her back.

"It's every man for himself out there."

"Exactly," muttered Isobel.

"Totally," said Helen.

"But she's in a wheelchair," muttered Sheryl. "Masked."

George and Sandy stared into a sea of children catching and chasing helium balloons, doing their best to burst each one, while who was left of the audience were filming on their mobiles.

On the flat-screen, to the sound of a brass band, was a video of Beatrice, clutching her petition, chasing a workman across the Kilmory car park. It was running at double speed, on a loop like a GIF.

The walls of gratitude were sliding open, hitting whatever was in the way and sliding back shedding photos like unwanted hair. By the nursery door was the nursery assistant, watching her manager in six-inch heels trying to round up children like a shepherd without a dog.

And by the kitchen door was McTaggart, red-faced, trying to retrieve his leaflets from children shuffling them about like cards.

A helium balloon exploded.

The manager jumped. "Jesus."

"Annabel?" said McTaggart in a high-pitched voice. "Can you not give us a hand?"

The manager raced to his aid as a pile of children pulled him under. Like the captain of a sinking ship, he went down, tumbling along with a wall of gratitude, his pop-up show, and his credibility . . .

All that was left was a hand, clutching a pop-up leaflet, outstretched from beneath a wall of gratitude.

"Aren't you going to help?" yelled the manager to the assistant.

The assistant, feigning deafness, retreated into the classroom to tidy.

And in the corner, George spied what had to be Beatrice.

"Is that a pumpkin and a penis?" said Sandy.

"Tombstone," muttered George.

Beatrice had no idea the extent of Ms Frasier's plans. She had no idea that Ms Frasier had squirrelled away photos of her and covered the walls of gratitude with them, not to mention tampered with the surveillance video.

She should have seen it coming the moment she saw that look on Ms Frasier's face and heard "accordion player."

But she didn't. She was too busy supervising the gluing of egg boxes; too busy creating a giant F-ing penis that she could hardly move in . . .

Beatrice looked at the video, the photos littered across the floor, her so-called comrade crumbled under the feet of children, and thanked God and all who served her that she still had her mask on . . .

"This was not my plan," muttered Ms Frasier as an accordion player at the entrance of the community centre began to play . . .*Campbeltown Loch.*

"Shit, I forgot about him," muttered Ms Frasier.

Retreat, thought Beatrice, *is the only option.*

Chapter Thirteen

THE BONFIRE

Never drink whisky with water. What's the good of starting a good fire and then putting it out with water?

A few days later, Beatrice was staring at a bonfire, tossing egg boxes in one at a time, when George appeared.

"You ready?" he said.

"Just a few more," she said, Frisbee-ing her mask into the flames.

They were heading to Sandy's.

Sandy was cooking a meal for her parents, a meal to celebrate the birthday of all birthdays, and afterwards, the family were going to watch, yet again, the video.

They had seen it a few times but still loved to watch. Even Sandy's husband enjoyed it—it was way better than any party.

Sky, who had videoed Beatrice's "Taj debacle," filmed the whole "pop-up/birthday incident" despite her mother's orders.

Sky had learnt from her zooming-in-and-out mistakes, mastering the art of filming that had many, including her teacher, calling her a genius.

In fact, so impressed was the teacher with her filming that she had arranged to include Sky's work in future media studies—in the high school.

Sky's film captured the beginning, the middle, and the end with, to quote her teacher, accuracy and poignancy, along with a high level of comic intuition. Even Sky's mother couldn't argue with that.

She filmed the front, back, and side of Beatrice wobbling through the car park like a stack of Lego bricks, the downfall of McTaggart along with the walls of gratitude, Sheryl's "Oh shit, it's children," the hurtling of Ms Frasier slim body, and the birthday boy's entrance—Frank's *favourite*—and finally ended with a poignant shot of Ms Frasier staring into the mess muttering, "If only I'd measured . . ."

Frank was under the impression that not only had the wool *not* been pulled over his eyes but he had saved the day.

No one had the heart to argue.

Frank arrived minutes after Beatrice's pondering about retreat. He, blocking her exit with his entourage of two, stopped and within seconds saw mayhem on a scale only seen in movies. He filled his lungs, ready for the bellowing of a lifetime, just as the children were heading for the kitchen.

Sky instinctively flashed her lens his way, zooming in on Frank's face, catching the flaring of his nostrils . . .

"What the *hell* is going on here?" he boomed . . .

The children stopped; the accordion whined to a long last chord as the kitchen door creaked open.

"Dad, you're early," muttered Sandy.

It always got a laugh . . .

"It was that tubby boy who was the leader of it all," said Frank. "As I said to my Princess Leia . . ."

"It's Sandy, Dad," said Sandy.

"Let him speak, Sandra," said Sandy's mother.

"It's Sandy, Mum."

"I sussed him, Princess . . ." Frank looked at his daughter.

"Sandy!" yelled Sandy.

"Sandra!" yelled Sandy's mother with one of her looks.

" . . . I saw him head for the kitchen," said Frank, "the others following. But I stopped 'em."

The truth was, it was Jabba.

The tubby boy saw it first and made the sort of fearful noise many would be ashamed of; soon others followed.

Once the children caught a glimpse of the eel-like eyes, the green shiny pastry, and the tail trailing around the table, oozing juices like a roast pig, they stopped. Was it alive, eatable, or both? They had no idea . . . let alone what or who it was.

Luke Skywalker was a mystery to them, let alone a gangster in the shape of a worm.

As they stared, wondering if it was about to move, Beatrice, still masked, entered, the slow whirl of her wheel cutting through the silence.

Bill, in the middle of picking up the photographs of Beatrice strewn across the floor, stopped to watch the wheelchair creeping into the kitchen.

"Jabba," she murmured through her mask, "eats little boys for breakfast one fingernail at a time. Then he starts on girls one by one, lick by lick."

Not a crumb was touched from that table until the candle was blown out, "Campbeltown Loch" was sung (accompanied by the accordion player), and the children, each clutching a stormtrooper cupcake, had left the building.

After their meal with Sandra, George took his time driving Beatrice home. She slid her hand on his thigh; he slipped on Jimmy Shand's "Campbeltown Loch" and smiled.

She hummed.

He laughed as he slid his hand on top of hers.

"Bill says you have guts of steel," said George.

"And you?" said Beatrice.

"Hmm . . . I can think of better things to talk about than your innards."

George drove into the drive, jumped out of the car, headed around to Beatrice's side, and opened the door.

"No cards this week, Francis is on holiday," he said.

"Who needs cards," she said, easing herself out, "when there's a bottle of good malt upstairs?"

They looked at each other. *And who needs fancy underpants?* they both thought.

EPILOGUE

*M*r McTaggart made it into the *Squeak* (the local newspaper), but not how he imagined. Mowed down by children is not something anyone would want to be famous for. McTaggart retired; one meeting with the other councillors was enough to convince him.

The pop-up library was never spoken of again, and the paperwork for the closure of the library was, thanks to Bill, taken from the pending tray and shredded. A meeting was held, and Bill, with a convincing "disabled access" argument, won the day.

"The chances of a wheelchair user using the gents in the community centre is as plausible as McTaggart singing nursery rhymes in the school," he said, swinging any undecided.

Bill's mother took one look at Beatrice's video and resurrected into the force he loved so much. She, a die-hard spoon player, decided there was still life in the old girl yet, and if Beatrice could entertain in a wheelchair, then so could she.

She turned up at the next storytelling event, ruined two of Beatrice's stories with her interpretation of suspense, and, after a lot of "mouthed swearing" between the two of them, left.

Bill's mother turned to bigger things, such as darts matches for those in wheelchairs and resurrecting Disability Week with Ms Frasier, until they fell out about the leaflets.

Ms Frasier continued her harassment of councillors, the latest issue being the bus timetables.

"If you can't get your buses to synchronize, then at least put more on" was the main thrust of her argument, put in so many ways that many fell asleep, stirred only by the ringing of mobiles . . .

And George, in the end, boxed his underpants up for the summer —a whole six months of glorious cuddling and laughing, with no pelvic swivelling—and for a while they wondered if they might forgo the whole card night . . . indefinitely.

I try to put the past behind me, yet there it is, in the dark places of my memory, erupting now and then like heartburn.

When I pick up a drum, all I can think about is playing it. It makes me so happy.

So happy that I'd laugh in the face of a phone queue, a flat tyre, a parking attendant. A parking attendant could give me a thousand tickets and I wouldn't give a flying fuck, as long as I have a drum to play.

Drumming does it for me; it's like illegal sex, sex that you shouldn't be doing. In fact, better than illegal sex, because I don't wake up in the morning feeling guilty.

Danny, my teacher, says I am a natural.

Steven says the only thing Danny can teach is how to drink. He says Danny's as much a teacher as he is a pole dancer.

Sheryl says I exaggerate like Beatrice, her mum, that I've been with her too long. And Beatrice?

Well, she thinks I'm a saint, she told me as much. But she doesn't know the real me. I'm no saint.

SAINT HELEN

I hadn't had sex for so long I felt androgynous, ugly, and boring. I hardly went out because I had little to wear that made me feel good, and all my friends simply loved Henry.

A few days after Beatrice's train wreck of a protest at the community centre, I helped her build a bonfire for the burning of the egg boxes. When I say *helped*, I mean *obeyed*, as she instructed like I had never built a bonfire before.

Her way took half a can of petrol, a packet of firelighters, and a few half-used candles from under the sink. The dust was probably more flammable than the ancient candles.

If Beatrice had listened to me, the fire would have gone up with a flick of a match, but one thing you learn when living within bossing distance of Beatrice is when to argue and when it's not worth the effort.

Sheryl says I'm way too patient with her mum.

The truth is, I don't have to take it. I can walk away any time and George would never be far behind with a decent whisky.

George was clutching one as we stood by the bonfire, a mile-high pile of egg boxes painted luminous greens and oranges. He, like me, was watching the egg boxes curl into the flames.

He pulled out a hip flask, took a sip, and then handed it to me, a delectable malt which warmed the whole of my body.

I began to ponder the eggs and hens. There must have been more than a hundred eggs that filled those boxes . . .

"All that hen's hard laying," I muttered.

"Aye," muttered George.

"It's enough to put you off eggs," I added.

"What?" said Beatrice.

"I said it's enough to put you off eggs."

"Hmmm," she muttered, staring at her mask like it had something to say and she had something to say after. "I'll never glue an egg box again—as long as I live," she said.

"But you didn't," said George. "Sheryl and Helen did."

"And as for a mask, the only one that will touch this face from now on is cosmetic"—she looked at me—"and I hear an egg white is good for that."

I said nothing.

"Take that, Ms Fraser," she shouted, and with a ceremonial toss, the mask landed on the other side of the fire and rolled onto the grass. The bright orange face stared up at the stars, almost daring us to try again.

George picked it up and with a grunt hurled it into the centre; the fire embraced it within seconds.

We watched in silence as the mask disappeared into the flames.

"That'll be that then," muttered George with a quiet sip of his whisky.

"To bigger things," toasted Beatrice.

"Bigger things," toasted George.

"And the hens," I said as Puss appeared by my leg and wrapped her tail around it.

It was a moving moment.

A moving moment broken by the flick of the patio light and a "right, let's go" shout by Beatrice, followed by Beatrice's usual noisy getting-into-the-car carry-on and George's car revving.

Getting into the car was a procedure for Beatrice that involved serious grunting, the odd command, and a fair amount of shouting. Her wheelchair weighed a ton, and it required the expertise of a

Rubik's Cube master to fold up and an empty boot to fit into—often the driver was caught off guard.

By the time they left for Sandy's to watch the "Downfall of Mr McTaggart" video *yet again,* my mellow mood had sunk into the sunset.

I could have gone, but I was thinking seriously about hens, eggs, and the whole animal-eating thing, and Sandy was planning a barbecue.

I pulled up a chair, poured another whisky, and watched as the sun went down and flames demolished everything into a pile of red ash.

It took a while for the mood to return.

Puss, in her sphinx pose, stared at me with her usual low hum of a purr, then jumped onto my knee like she knew what I was thinking.

"Enough with all this meat-and-dairy stuff," I yelled into the fire.

She pushed her head into my hand for a stroke and blinked mid purr, and I'm pretty sure I detected a smile, a "good on yer, luv."

Either way, she arched her back with a stretch, then with a seductive meow began winding into a ball on my legs, followed by some serious kneading.

I watched her settle into a purring ball of contentment.

Yes, that's it, definitely no animal stuff from now on. I thought and texted my pal Sheryl.

"No more bacon rolls for me," I texted, "I'm giving it all up, going vegan."

We were working the next day, and the last thing I needed was her arriving with one of Steven's delicious bacon creations. They had been my downfall many times.

The next morning, I emptied my fridge of all things animally, creating a monster of a sandwich around leftover turkey. I jumped into Sheryl's van, cracking an old giblet joke which I can't for the life of me remember now, and hurled the sandwich her way.

We were heading to a job.

"Here," I said. "No more meat for me, you have it."

With a quick inspection, she handed it back. "I hate turkey."

"It's a damn fine sandwich, a work of art." I handed it back to her. "That mayo is Beatrice's finest."

She tossed it into my lap. "Still hate turkey. Why don't you eat it?"

"I'm going vegan," I said.

"Oh," said Sheryl, "forgot about that."

"I took one look at Puss," I said, "and thought, 'You're a dinner in Thailand.'"

"I think that's dogs," muttered Sheryl. She stopped. "Why don't you eat it and then go vegan?"

"I can't," I said. "Once you've turned, you can't go back."

"Like milk," muttered Sheryl.

Ignoring her milk comment, I went on to talk of my "leg-in-the-bath epiphany," a moment when I looked down at my thigh and thought it was "just like a chicken drumstick." I was halfway through before realising I was repeating myself, but as I had started, I continued.

"Meat on a bone," I finished.

"Your leg would hardly feed a cat they're so thin," said Sheryl.

I laughed. "That's what your Mum said. She seems to think my turning to lentils is a personal stab at her and her bacon rolls."

"They're enough to turn anyone vegan," muttered Sheryl.

"So I told her if being vegan is good enough for Danny, then it's good enough for me."

Sheryl looked at me. "Danny the alcoholic?"

"He's given up the drink, along with meat," I said. "'Digging the beats and cruising with the veg,' he calls it."

"Can't see him eating lentils," muttered Sheryl.

"He's a changed man," I said.

"And what about cauliflower cheese?" said Sheryl. "How can you survive without real cheese?"

"Full of hormones," I said. "Apparently, vegans don't get hot flushes."

Sheryl looked at the sandwich, pulled it open, sniffed, and, after an admiring glance at the mayo, pushed the sandwich back together and slid it onto my lap.

"Why don't you give it to Puss?" she said, which in the end I did.

Puss sniffed at the mayo, jolted back like it was somehow electrified, tentatively moved towards it like it was going to pounce, sniffed again, pushed it with her paws, and then, with a glare at me, walked away like she was way too royal for such leftovers covered in mayo.

DRUMS AND SPOONS

As you get older, your face becomes a road map.

Danny lived in a house with no cats or dogs, just mice droppings. I went there once for a drumming lesson and decided we would meet at mine in the future. I was seriously suspicious about the tea . . . the mug . . . along with whatever I was sitting on . . . not to mention the smell.

I didn't ask either. I suspected Danny, by the look of his home, had lost the art of smelling years ago.

He wasn't a bad old bloke—when he was off the drink—but obviously not good enough to, you know, clean up.

He must have been about seventy or more, with the cough of a miner who had spent a lifetime on roll-ups. He was thin, like a wet cat, with hair stuck to his skull fine enough to see his skull beneath and a chin whiskery enough to see what he last ate, but you forgot all that once he played the drums.

We held three classes in the garage under my flat and were planning on more, until he met the Bag Lady who lives in a teepee in Neff's garden.

They met the day after the bonfire, by the automatic checkout in the co-op. I, with a basket of lentils and beans, watched Danny, with a carton of orange juice and several jumbo packets of crisps, try to master the automatic till. He was just passing a pack of salt and vinegar through for the third time when the Bag Lady appeared, clutching a packet of firelighters at the next auto cashier.

Danny now an expert offered to help.

Soon they were talking of drums and campfires and had arranged a "jamming session," which had Neff on the phone to Sheryl, moaning about "unknown men loitering about" and how "no musician could be trusted."

We had finished work for the day and were packing up the tools in the garage under my flat when Sheryl's phone pinged with a "phone me" message from Neff.

Sheryl spent an hour on the phone pulling a series of eye-rolls, while I, unpacking tools, did my best to interpret.

After two eye-rolls, I had worked out it wasn't her mum, and by the time I had the tools sorted for the next day, I knew it was Neff on the phone and a bonfire was in the offing, despite Neff's conviction that Danny's intentions were anything but honourable.

Beatrice, with a sniff, said it was a bad idea; she had a thing about Neff and didn't want me, a "too kind for my own good" sort of person, under the influence.

She thought I was the sort of person people "take a lend of," and every day she told me as much.

I hadn't the heart to disappoint.

I've done things that would make a better person cringe, that I have never told anyone—that keep me awake at night. I try to put the past behind me, and yet my friggin' past lingers like the smell of a fart, taunting me.

Sometimes I forget, like when I am drumming or dealing with Beatrice, cooking her something she is going to sniff like it's past its sell-by date. I begin to feel okay, that I'm not a bad person, and then my memories hit me, jolt me like a slap across the chops, and I am overwhelmed with guilt.

"The last place you need to be is with that so-called belly dancer," said Beatrice.

"Mum, she *is* a belly dancer," said Sheryl.

"At her age?" said Beatrice.

"What's age got to do with it?" I said. "It never stopped you."

"I am of the age where it doesn't matter," said Beatrice. "I have reached and passed her age years ago. I've earned the right to throw *it* all to the wind. She is a few years away from *that* privilege."

"It?" Sheryl looked at me. "What is *it*?"

"Well you know, *it . . . stuff . . .*"

I stopped. "Stuff?"

"You know . . ." Beatrice huffed.

We looked at her.

"Swinging her bits at her age, who wants to see that?" said Beatrice.

"Bits?" said Sheryl.

"Yes, you know, *bits;* she decorates her bits and then . . . well . . . gyrates," said Beatrice. "Like Kylie Minogue. Except she's not Kylie, is she?"

"Well no," Sheryl and I muttered.

"And gyrating is not the sort of thing a woman collecting a pension should do."

"Gyrate?" Sheryl laughed. "You've never been bothered about gyrating before."

"What about Madonna?" I said.

Beatrice shivered. "Oooh, I hate her. She's not human, let alone a woman, she's a yoga machine. Anyone with arms like that can gyrate all they want, it'll never give rise to anything. It's just the gays that watch her."

"Cher? You like her, and she wears less than a stripper," said Sheryl.

"She's more my vintage," said Beatrice, "and I don't think she gyrates anymore."

"You're talking bollocks, Mum," said Sheryl.

"You just don't like Neff," I said, "and you're making excuses."

At which point Beatrice left.

Steven met us at the garden with Baby Bea and a bag full of food. The Bag Lady, who was looking quite sparkly, had arranged the seating around the fire, which was way bigger than her usual fire in a coal scuttle.

Danny was already there in a clean checked shirt, matching socks, and no whiskers, sipping "the finest stewed tea ever!"

Apparently, he'd been there for ages, helping with the fire.

Danny can beat out a rhythm on anything; give him a spanner and an oil drum and he'll have your feet tapping in minutes. His limbs pulsate rhythm, and they're constantly on the go. A spoon isn't a spoon to him, neither is a mug a mug, but rather a new instrument to explore. Sitting in a coffee shop with Danny is like sitting opposite a teenager with headphones on pulsing rhythm from music you have no idea of.

Danny sees life in beats.

As I arrived, he was in the midst of explaining Egyptian rhythms to the Bag Lady. He brought his Egyptian drums to play in honour of Neff, who he claimed to have seen dance at least once . . .

The Bag Lady, with her African drum, was trying to follow along with Betty, her best pal, who, with a couple of spoons, was cheesing the Bag Lady off with her lack of rhythm.

Dum tak tak . . . dum tak—Danny drumming.

Beat . . . beat . . . beat-beat beat . . . beat—the Bag Lady drumming.

Clank . . . clank . . . click-ity, click-ity, click-ity . . . Clank—Betty on spoons . . .

"Give me those spoons," snapped the Bag Lady.

"My spoon playing is the talk of the steamie," said Betty.

"The steamie is well gone," snapped the Bag Lady, "and there was never any playing of spoons there."

"What about some sticks?" said Danny.

He caught my eye as I entered with Steven and Sheryl.

"Hey, man, good to see you," he said.

Sheryl and Steven, taken aback by Danny clean, sober, and smiling, stopped.

"Danny?"

Neff arrived soon after; she'd just finished her shift at the Indian.

She stood at the back door clutching a bag of pakoras and was about to shout something when she caught sight of Danny mid drumming a Saudi beat . . .

Dum tak, dum dum tak . . .

She stopped. "Danny?"

Dum tak, dum dum tak . . .

"Aye, it's Danny," shouted the Bag Lady. "Have you not seen a man in a checked shirt before?"

"Well yes," shouted Neff.

Danny stopped . . .

"But not Danny."

Soon, Neff was up dancing with Sheryl, giving Betty, who had given up on the sticks, a few tips.

Dum tak, dum dum tak . . .

I had no idea that Amy would turn up looking like she did. Like she had had the sort of conversation with her father I had often dreaded . . .

Beatrice, it seemed, had told her where I was.

Chapter Sixteen

SECRETS

You can say "no" to ninety-nine men, and the one you didn't is the one you're remembered for, the one that earned you the name "slut" when you're caught—and you are always, in the end, caught.

When Amy was born, I fell in love straight away. She was the most beautiful being I had ever seen. Her smooth round head mesmerised me as I fed her, as did the first time she looked up at me and smiled.

Henry claimed he wanted a son, but when Amy was born, he seemed satisfied, and over the years he developed an "I'm busy but you're cute" head-patting sort of relationship with his daughter. The old-fashioned-father sort of relationship where grunting meant "okay" and "getting into trouble" meant an overreaction of mega proportions.

He claimed he wanted more children, but one look at a dirty nappy had him gagging like a chicken bone had caught in his throat, and as for pushing a pram, he'd rather sort a burst sewage pipe than be seen with his daughter.

He left everything to me—the feeding, the doctor visits, the parent-teacher nights—and then when things went wrong, there was an explosion of violence: walls smashed, clean washing tossed in the mud, mugs hurled across the room. It was always my fault when Amy didn't sleep, became unwell, or, worse still, got into trouble at school.

The first bad school report Amy brought home I hid from Henry, until he bumped into the teacher in the co-op. His rage was so bad he kicked the garden gnome into the field opposite. There it lay for days, its decapitated head poking out from our neighbours' compost heap.

I don't know if Amy saw, but she said little . . .

Henry had a knack of taking his temper out on things that I loved, usually out of earshot of Amy.

Nothing fazed Amy.

She was an amazing little girl who chatted little but was always by my side, holding my hand, until oestrogen hit . . . and she turned into a teenager and started slamming doors and rolling her eyes. By then our house was always full of Henry's friends, drinking. It was easy to lie, to hide her teenage antics from his temper. By then I was good at lying to Henry, anyway: I had developed the knack for cheating.

The first time I cheated on Henry, my ex-husband, I was completely taken by surprise. It was a snog in a dark corner of a pub, the teenage sort that leaves your lips red and swollen and your fanny aching. The sort that had me waking up in the morning surprised I was still alive, that the earth hadn't caved in, and Henry had no idea . . .

When I first met Henry, I hadn't much idea about sex other than the odd fumble in the car. At first it was magnificent, leaving me with a glow.

Until I fell pregnant . . .

Everything changed. For a start, we had to move from a caravan to a home, which, looking back, didn't exactly make Henry jump for joy. He was busy building other folks' houses and had no time for us . . . and suddenly he had to find time. I think he begrudged me all the attention a pregnant woman attracts.

He began to make jokes, calling me "Whale Woman" and "Big Jessie," claiming that it would be easier to climb Mount Everest than mount my stomach.

The funny thing was, people laughed, even women; he had a way of making an insult funny, and as I ballooned into pregnancy, his jokes expanded, and every sexual feeling I felt died.

I don't think Henry ever got over seeing Amy born, either; somehow my bits were never as allusive. Everything went completely off the boil. He just couldn't find any bit of my body attractive enough to touch.

"One look at you and my dick deflates like a balloon," he said, and when I looked in the mirror, I couldn't help but agree with him.

It took about a year before we had a "go." It was at a family wedding, and I was drunkenly tucking into egg sandwiches like I hadn't eaten for weeks. He was staring at the yolks tumbling onto my dress, and the next thing I knew I was whisked away to a car and given a good seeing to.

The fear of being caught turned him on.

Soon he was banging on about outdoor adventures, parking lots, or the latest building site where he was working. Henry's idea of foreplay was to call me for a viewing of his handywork.

"Come up and see my plastering," he'd say.

Code for "hard-on: attention needed." With a drill in one hand and a mastic gun in another, he'd show me his hard work, expecting me to feel erotic amongst the rubble and plywood, like somehow admiring his handiwork would get me all juicy. He thought romance was the smell of damp and fear of getting caught, along with his roll-on roll-off in-and-out method.

He seemed oblivious to my feelings, the fact that my body felt pain, or the need for foreplay. He hadn't kissed me since Maggie Thatcher retired, let alone touched me, and my fanny, it seemed, had packed up and gone to the Bahamas. There wasn't a delicious feeling left . . .

Soon, I began to wonder why I'd married Henry. I felt nothing; sex had turned into a grunting affair that I dreaded.

And I began to make excuses . . .

There is nothing worse than shit sex, the sort that has you staring at the ceiling waiting for it to end while your partner bangs away like a toddler on a drum, too drunk for anything to happen. Henry blamed me for the *shit* sex, claiming that I "grabbed his penis like a toothbrush."

I was so grateful when the sex stopped . . .

Grateful when Henry stopped asking me to visit his workplace and in fact insisted on me not coming around. Grateful when Henry started coming home late, smelling different, sometimes of perfume or aftershave.

It was a relief to go to bed untouched, left alone, until one day in my forties, when I thought everything down there had shriveled up, I was touched again . . .

Don't get me wrong, I didn't wallow. I went out, laughed, drank, flirted when I got the chance, even wore makeup the odd time.

Sometimes I felt okay.

Sometimes I even tried to talk to someone about how shit things were, but when your pals have partners that walk in the door and say "hi" and who pick up milk on the way home when asked, who take turns to drink and drive, it's hard for that pal to understand what it's like to be married to a man who would rather have a hernia operation than coffee with his wife. Especially when the same man can be seen washing dishes for his aunt and mending flat tyres for old ladies.

Henry was one of those men who was generous and funny to strangers and blondes, a laugh a minute to his workmates, a confidant to his mates' wives, and abusive to the one who made his mince and tatties.

In the end, I drank more and laughed like a madwoman; when I escaped for the night, I went crazy, never wanting to go back, getting in at dawn like some sort of party animal.

Sex is on a plate late at night, especially when the wine is flowing. Of course, it's easy to laugh in the face of a drunk, to say no to a man who's as likely to manage a shag as walk a straight line. It's much harder when the man offering you a good time is half your age and looking at you like you are the only woman on the planet, especially when he looks like he can not only walk a straight line but draw it.

And what makes it harder—almost impossible—to say "no" is when you're gagging for affection, attention, or even just a listening ear, and the only thing you have to go home to is a man who'd rather have his balls waxed than look at your body. Then, saying no takes all the willpower you can muster, along with a decent reason why you're turning down the shag of a lifetime, apart from the fact that your knickers belong in the dustbin.

I said no to a lot—ninety-nine percent—just not a hundred, and the first time for me was as addictive as an addict's first trip.

Until I backed the wrong horse, did *it* with the worst man possible, and made a complete mess of things.

Chapter Seventeen

PERFECT EYEBROWS

Being unfaithful is not something to indulge in if you have a guilt complex; only a narcissist walks away guilt-free.

The first time, I was sitting in the pub watching my darts team lose when in walked two young men. One eyed me straight away. We immediately clicked, and after several drinks, we were laughing like best buddies. The next thing I knew, we were in a dark corner snogging like teenagers, me wishing I'd left the pork scratchings alone.

He'd grabbed me as I walked out of the ladies', taken me by surprise. I thought he liked my jokes, my banter; it never occurred to me that what was underneath my jumper was what he was really interested in.

His hands were everywhere, and I, parked against the wall, didn't put up a fight. I was too busy marvelling at the delicious feelings inside me and how great it was to have a tongue inside my mouth which knew what to do. My nipples tingled so much it was all I could do not to make a noise; in fact, trying not to make a noise made it even sexier.

We snogged for ages, so long that the bar closed; the lights clicked off, and we, whispering and laughing, slid out the fire door . . .

Much later, I slid into bed next to Henry, snoring with Tripod our cat on his chest. (She only had three legs, hence the name—a Henry witticism.)

Tripod blinked as I stretched onto my back, then jumped off with a thud. The house was silent, the sun was coming up. I stared at Tripod's silhouette by the window . . .

Did that really happen? I thought.

Henry let out a snore, a "Put 'em down" mumble . . . followed by a punch in the air.

I pushed him onto his side . . .

What the hell was the snogger's name? I wondered.

The next day, I woke to hear Henry head out the door, start the car, and leave.

I stretched out in the bed as Tripod landed on my stomach and meowed a "feed me" into my face; cat food made Henry gag like a dog with worms.

Did it really happen, I thought, *or was it a drunken dream?*

I stroked Tripod, and she, with an unimpressed look, meowed louder. I looked at myself in the mirror and there it was: a hickey—a love bite—the size of a doorknob on my neck . . .

Shit.

I stroked it, turned my head to see a line of them lower down. *What the hell was his name?*

I was filled with a strange mixture of disbelief, relief, and, despite a hangover, energy. What I had done against a wall I had never managed in a bed before, and not once did he hurt; in fact, he was very gentle in a masterly sort of way and everything it seemed was still in working order.

I vowed never again; I wasn't that sort of woman. I had a cat and a daughter to think of and a husband who threw tantrums over such catastrophes as lumpy mash; what was I thinking?

Never again, I told myself when I looked in the mirror, jumped in the car, stared at Henry dozing, *no more "snogs with no names" for me.* But turning down that feeling again was not such an easy pill to digest; despite the guilt, it had been so delicious . . .

Do I really want to spend the rest of my life with a fanny as redundant as a Welsh miner? Live on a memory of a nameless snog?

I decided to buy a vibrator.

I had seen a couple of them at a hen party humping about a table like legless dicks, and I, like many, had flashed a glance at an Ann Summers window, sometimes stopping for a better look . . .

Ann Summers is the sort of shop that sells sex toys and lingerie for women, and I had passed it many times. Well, this time, I wasn't going to fanny about—I was going in.

Sexual pleasure was not something talked about when I grew up, only the importance of virginity and how once it was lost you were as soiled as yesterday's knickers.

"There were two types of women," my dad used to say, "those ridden like a bike and those men cleaned cars for and took home to their mother."

Henry stopped cleaning my car years ago, and his mother lived in South Africa. Meeting her was like meeting the Gestapo; I spent the whole time holding my already flat stomach in and trying not to swear, until she dropped a biscuit and the dog gulped it in one go.

She slapped the dog with the sort of venom that had me feeling for Henry. "Fucking hell!" she yelled as Henry cringed.

Thank God she'd moved to South Africa.

It was a Monday morning when I walked in. Ann Summers was empty apart from two assistants lounging about the counter talking about their holidays.

They clocked me straight away as I lingered by the edible body paint . . .

The older assistant nudged her comrade as I picked up a pink tube of "pussy rub" and tried to read the label without my glasses. She was mid-forties and had a blonde hairdo with short back and sides, six-inch heels, and glasses swinging from a gold chain just shy of a cleavage that would have Henry cracking Mount Everest jokes.

"VV at eleven o'clock," chuckled Short Back and Sides, setting her cleavage into motion.

Her younger male comrade's perfect eyebrows twitched. "What was that, Darl?"

"Vibrator virgin," laughed Short Back and Sides.

Perfect Eyebrows flashed a smile with uniform Hollywood teeth. There was not a wrinkle in sight.

I moved towards the back of the shop as they watched. It was a bit unnerving, but I was determined. I picked up a set of handcuffs, pondering the dark corner of the pub . . . and fumbled.

"Definitely a first," muttered Perfect Eyebrows.

I caught sight of several vibrators arranged like a selection of James Bond weapons at HQ. I, mid wondering if Q would appear, fingered a silver bullet-shaped object. I turned it about in my hands.

It looked like it would fit . . .

"What do you reckon, the Rabbit?" said Short Back and Sides.

Rabbit? I stopped . . .

"Always the Rabbit, dear." Perfect Eyebrows laughed. "Need any help, luv?" he shouted across to me.

I stopped. "Well . . . I . . . err . . . not sure . . ."

Chapter Eighteen

THE RABBIT

Lubricant is a girl's best friend.

With a Marilyn Monroe saunter, Perfect Eyebrows appeared beside me, followed by the clipped march of Short Back and Sides.

I fumbled about with words, trying to describe what I was looking for, and they watched like a toddler pulling wings off a fly.

"I was sort of wondering . . ." I muttered.

"What, luv?" said Perfect Eyebrows.

"About getting . . ." I faltered. "It's just that . . . well."

"Hmmm?" they said in unison like two Gothic undertakers.

"It's my first time . . ." I blurted.

"Bit overwhelming, pet?" Perfect Eyebrows flashed his teeth.

"There's so many . . ."

"I know." He patted my arm.

". . . sizes, shapes, and colours," I muttered. "That one"—I gestured with the silver bullet—"looks like it'd block a toilet, let alone . . ." I attempted a chuckle. "Down below."

"It's all in the shape," said Short Back and Sides, casting a glance at her comrade.

"And lubricant," muttered Perfect Eyebrows.

Lubricant? I thought.

I looked about. There were things I had never seen before: G strings that looked as comfortable as a G string, shiny tight nurse and Santa outfits looking as comfortable as, well . . . as a G string, oils that promise the impossible and enough flavoured condoms to fill a sweet shop.

"We've all been there, luv," he said.

I stared down at the silver bullet in my hand.

"Do they all . . . you know . . . fit?" I said.

Short Back and Sides eyed my lean frame. "Anything would fit you."

"No, I meant those." I waved the bullet at the vibrators on show. "Never used one before."

"Always a first time," said Short Back and Sides, swiftly lifting the bullet from me with a *way out of your league* sniff. "We'll soon sort you out."

She marched towards the stand like she was missing a whip and someone had hidden it. She, gesturing for me to follow, pulled out a large pink dildo and waved it under my nose. The smell of *new* lingered.

"Beginners," she said in a clipped fashion. "Durable, flexible, and easy to clean."

"I don't want anything too noisy," I muttered.

"Of course, dear," said Short Back and Sides.

"I mean I've seen them in a porn . . . err . . . film."

They looked at me.

"Not that I'm a regular watcher," I laughed, "just the odd, you know . . . when I was younger; curious . . . like."

"Ooh seventies—natural pubes," chuckled Perfect Eyebrows.

"More eighties," I muttered.

I looked at Short Back and Sides, woman to woman.

"*Mission: Impossible*." I chuckled. "I mean if I saw that before I was married . . ."

She hushed me with her hand. "This is what I use when my boyfriend's away, and I've tried everything . . ."

"She's tried 'em all," Perfect Eyebrows jumped in.

"But honestly," said Short Back and Sides, "I always go back to my Rabbit."

"She's lost without it," said Perfect Eyebrows, "been through at least . . ." He silently counted. *Four? Five?*

Short Back and Sides threw him a look, then turned to me. "Honestly, there is no substitute. If I don't get my weekly—"

"Weekly? Pfff—daily, more like it," said Perfect Eyebrows. "When I stayed with you, I needed earplugs."

"Daily?" I said.

Short Back and Sides glared at her comrade.

"We're all girls here," he said to her, then touched my arm. "If you saw *him* you'd have a few Rabbits too."

"Him?" I said.

"Oh absolutely you'd have a draw full," said Perfect Eyebrows.

I looked at Short Back and Sides.

"He's talking about my boyfriend," sighed Short Back and Sides.

"A beard like a Taliban," said Perfect Eyebrows.

Short Back and Side pulled a face.

"I'd go crazy if he went down there with that thing," said Perfect Eyebrows.

"Jesus," she muttered.

"I mean honestly I would." He pulled a face.

"We're not here to talk about what you like," she said.

Perfect Eyebrows shivered. "Hate beards."

Short Back and Side threw him a *shut it* look.

"Well I'm sorry, luv, but his must prickle like a cactus," he said.

"There is nothing cactus-y about my Lenard," snapped Short Back and Sides.

"Even the name gives me prickles." Perfect Eyebrows shivered again.

"Yes, well, lucky for you he's not your type, is he?"

Short Back and Sides looked at me. "He just loves eighties-style butch men . . . packed at the front like one of your porn films."

"Only watched one years ago," I muttered.

"I'm just a tart," laughed Perfect Eyebrows, "but who cares? It's not like we're gonna live forever."

"Don't be saying such things," she said.

He looked at me. "She's vegan, thinks it will make a difference—save the panda, the white leopard, the whale, the whole friggin' world."

"If we all gave up meat," she said, "then—"

"There'd be enough rice for everyone," snapped Perfect Eyebrows. "Yeah, well, honey, rice gives me wind."

I turned to her. "I'm a vegan." *Well, thinking of it . . .*

"No worries here." She threw me a warm smile. "Even the lubricant's animal-free"—she tapped my arm—"and gluten-free as well."

Twenty minutes later, I, clutching my "this is not from Ann Summer's" bag, walked out of Ann Summers filled with expectation, at least two great stories to entertain Sheryl and the brother with, a decent set of underpants that I was assured was comfortable, and an "easy as sliced vegan cheese" vegan sausage recipe.

Not that I had anyone to wear lacy lingerie for, but as Perfect Eyebrows said, "You never know when a car will come along and knock you over"—*which had Short Back and Sides tutting*—"and darling, the last thing you need when a handsome nurse casts his eyes across your smalls is to be seen in a set a bag lady would sling in the bin."

I was so excited I began to wonder about face cream and teeth whitener—really treating myself—and I was just heading for the pound shop when I heard my name shouted across the street.

I looked up to see Richie waving with a young fella beside him . . . with a face familiar. I had seen it before, but where?

Richie was Henry's best friend. I'd known him for years, and I watched as he played the field, chatting up women with warm eyes, laughing in all the right places. He was considered a catch. His parents owned the Ferry Inn, a farm, and several holiday cottages; Richie could work when it suited him, and he had a girlfriend, Wendy, who was miles away and always looked miserable when she visited.

Over the years, he had brought Henry home when too drunk to stand, eaten loads of meals with us, and treated Amy like a niece. It was he who persuaded Henry to go to school concerts and calmed him down when Henry exploded over Amy's teenage antics. Richie made being married to Henry easier, bearable.

It took a few stares and a wave for it all to come back, for me to recognise just where I knew the *other* face from . . .

It was the "Snog with No Name," and his face was empty as my reply.

I gulped.

He looked like a boy . . .

Chapter Nineteen

THE TALE OF TWO SHAGS

Once the deed is done, the name is often irrelevant.

Sheryl laughed her head off when I told her about Ann Summers, making thin jokes about wet wipes and returned vibrators and offering to "go back" together.

Then, when I told her about bumping into Richie, she nearly peed herself. According to her Wendy was as interested in vibrators as she was moving to Scotland.

"I swear he knew what I had bought," I said. "It was like he was daring me to open the bag."

Snog with No Name said nothing.

"This is Helen," Richie said to Snog with No Name. Snog with No Name eyed me and my Ann Summers bag behind me and with a blank face said, "We've already met."

Richie laughed out loud, stopping a few shoppers, and then, along with Snog with No Name, headed off, me still with no idea who the hell Snog with No Name was . . .

I did find out what rugby team he supported, the position he played in his college rugby team—*oh God, still a student*—and what he liked at McDonald's, because he was polishing it off like he hadn't eaten in days.

A few days later, thanks to Richie, I found out his name . . .

Richie and his girlfriend Wendy had announced their engagement to a room full of people celebrating impending Christmas.

"We're getting married," said Richie, while Wendy flashed a ring the size of a bath plug; they looked as happy as a hangover, liked they had picked the winning lottery numbers for the wrong week.

There was a mild cheer and a few confused looks. No one expected it; they just assumed Richie would be permanently single.

I know I did.

Wendy was an enigma. When I first met her, she was sitting in the corner of a room, shy and alone, while Richie entertained the crowd. There was a general feeling of disappointment in Richie's choice of woman, and I felt for her, until I got to know her. I tried to be friends, prise some sort of conversation out of her, but Wendy had a moan for everything and the ability to listen on par with a toddler's. Spending time with her required a decent amount of whisky and an ability to fall asleep with your eyes open. She only lit up when Amy was in the room.

"It'll not last," muttered an ol' boy at the party. "They should be all over each other."

"Anyone would think they were brother and sister," muttered another.

I shouldn't have listened; it gave me false hope.

There was a mountain of drink that evening, and by the end of the night, Henry was well oiled and had to be walked home. Wendy insisted that Richie help me, and as he did, he made jokes about Ann Summers and rugby-playing students playing other fields.

He was as cryptic as Snow White.

"Take Andy," he said.

"Andy?"

"Yes, Andy—you know, the young guy the other day in front of Ann Summers," said Richie.

"Oh, him . . ." I acted casual.

"He puts it about like a rabbit."

"Like a tup at tupping time," slurred Henry.

"I see," I said.

"He's a thing for older women," said Richie.

"Is that right," I said.

"Can't beat experience," Henry said, stumbling.

I grabbed him.

"Stick 'em up," shouted Henry with another stumble.

Richie grabbed the other side. Our eyes met . . .

"He's just playing the field," muttered Richie.

"Right," I said.

"Aye right!" shouted Henry. "Playing the field, that's rugby for yer . . . on a fucking field!"

"He's not something you can, you know . . . rely on," said Richie.

I said nothing.

"As fly as a fucking fly," jeered Henry.

"I get the picture," I said.

We stumbled up the road; it was rough and hilly. Henry grunted, punched the air a few times, and then called Richie "the best thing since sliced bread, sliced fucking cheese, and Dairylea."

"Isn't that cheese too?" Richie said with a wink at me.

"There's cheese and there's cheese, and you're the Dairylea of 'em all," Henry slurred.

We slipped Henry onto the bed and I took off his shoes.

Henry patted my head like he was hammering in a nail.

I pulled away.

Richie looked into my eyes.

"Aye right enough!" Henry punched the air again as Richie tossed a blanket over him.

He looked at me and smiled.

Henry let out a loud snore.

"Thanks," I said.

"That's what friends are for," he whispered.

And I stupidly believed him.

A few days later, I was preparing the turkey for Christmas the next day and up to my arms in apricot stuffing and bread sauce when Richie sauntered in like he always did. He had just dropped Wendy off at the airport and was looking hungry.

Richie spotted a dying fire in the lounge room and, midst joking with Amy, tried to resurrect it.

Amy was going through her "I'm not a tomboy anymore" phase. She'd gone from a chirpy wee thing in jeans and trainers to a silent stranger in skirts and heels. She got her hair cut, started wearing eyeliner and slamming doors, which Henry blamed on me, but she always cheered up when Richie walked in.

Soon he was in the kitchen looking for firelighters. He caught my eye and reached under the sink, and his hand lingered on my ankle.

It was like an electric shock.

I was stirring the bread sauce at the time; a clove shot out from the pan. He laughed and slid his hand onto my hip, where it stayed till Henry's car arrived.

I thought of his touch during Christmas, mulling over whisky, watching Henry carve the turkey, stirring gravy, and while putting Henry to bed yet again as he staggered in from spreading Christmas cheer to all in the village bar me, and for the first time in a year, through all the drunken festive season that usually had me wallowing in TV repeats and chocolates, I felt hope.

Richie and I had always been friends, great friends; I can't tell you how kind he could be. But I had no idea that he felt that way about me.

He had pretty much made the move on all the women in the village, but never me, which made me feel special, close to him.

What an idiot.

I should have stopped drinking, stopped hoping, and, most of all, turned to a pal with my disappointment, not to sex. But then when you really want something that's not yours to take, you hear what you want to hear and do whatever it takes to get it.

I brought posh face cream and teeth whitener and went through my underpants drawer, humming . . . waiting, wondering when he would touch me again.

I began to picture us together: me cleaning his holiday cottages, him walking in with coffee, testing out the beds . . .

No more lonely weekends, finally someone to talk to. We had a great friendship, we laughed, his face lit up when he saw me, he even loved my cooking. We were a match, I told myself; even Amy liked him. I pictured us as a family.

Guilt never entered my head.

After all, they weren't married *yet,* and Wendy had changed with each visit, becoming increasingly distant, cold, and calculating.

"When I first met Richie, I thought he was boring," she said. "I had no idea where he came from, until we drove up the drive of the hotel. I couldn't believe it—he owned all that." She laughed. "I'd put up with six months of shit for that."

He really loves me, I told myself, and I guess I kind of hoped he would save me.

Chapter Twenty

THE TABLA

The dum is the deep, rich sound, the backbone of the rhythm; the tak is lighter and lifts the rhythm, pushes it on . . .

I watched Amy enter the bonfire circle. She looked distracted, like she had something to say and yet didn't know how to begin.

She sat beside me, huddled close, at first saying little.

Over the years, Amy had turned from the outrageous teenager in heels and spiky short hair to an accountant, earning a decent living while her husband Gary worked as a chef. They'd met in Glasgow when Amy was a student and decided to move back to the area after the wedding, when Gary landed work in a local bistro and no longer had to work in the evenings.

For the first time in years, he would be home at night with Amy, and they, loved up, moved into a small place on the canal and took up fishing as Amy began to work from home. She was slowly building up her clients, and I absolutely loved having her nearby, even if it did mean putting up with the odd "Dad's the tits" comment.

After a couple of drinks, she nudged me. "Mum," she whispered. "I have heard something."

I nodded and waited.

"From Dad," said Amy. "He did his 'I have something to say and don't interrupt me till I'm finished' speech."

"I didn't know he had one," I muttered.

"Neither did I till he started," said Amy. "I told him I didn't want to hear any Mum-slagging."

I stopped. "He still slags me off?"

"Like a babbling brook," muttered Danny.

The Bag Lady chuckled.

"Well, sometimes." She threw Danny a look. "I think he's pissed you keep taking his jobs."

"And the rest," said Danny.

"We are cheaper," said Sheryl. She looked at me. "Usually."

"That's what he said," said Amy. "And he said he didn't mind, but the *Richie thing* really cheesed him off."

Richie thing? I thought. My heart began to beat fast; my stomach screwed up, twisted in knots, despite Neff's pakoras, as my mind went into overdrive . . . *Did Henry say something? I bet he did. I knew he would . . . bastard. Now Amy will hate me all over again . . . shit, shit, shit!*

"Richie thing?" I gulped.

"The hotel," said Amy.

"Oh, that—thank God." I sighed.

"Thank God?" Amy looked at me.

"I mean . . . well," I stuttered.

"If he can't fix a leak," jumped in Sheryl, "then what the fuck is he doing?"

"It's not really what I came to say," muttered Amy.

"I mean what plumber can't mend a friggin' leak?" said Sheryl.

"Loads," said Danny.

"He's not a plumber, he's a builder," said Amy.

"Your dad's an arsehole," said the Bag Lady. "It's not the first leak he's buggered up."

"It's not really about the leak," said Amy.

"Aye," said Betty. "Look what he did to my son's place. Needed new carpet."

"He's a builder, not a plumber, and besides, it's *not* about the leak," said Amy. "It's more . . . personal."

"Do you want us to go?" said Steven.

"Or you can go inside," said Neff.

"It's not *that* personal," said Amy.

"Oh," I muttered.

"And you'll hear soon enough anyway," said Amy.

Jesus, I thought.

"Spit it out, for Chrissake," shouted Danny.

"Dad's got a boyfriend," blurted Amy.

"What?" I said.

"Yes, and he's acting all, you know . . . stupid," said Amy. "Like he's in love or something."

I poured a drink. *Thank God . . .*

"I find that hard to believe," said Betty. "I mean he was always eyeing the women, chatting them up, even caught him once . . ." She stopped, looked at me. "It's not something I like to remember."

"And I wouldn't mind, but *he's* taken over my dad," said Amy, "just when we became, well, almost friends."

"It will blow over," said Sheryl.

"Blow over? Dad's all gooey and yuck," said Amy. "He's even painted the kitchen."

Betty turned to me. "Did you ever suspect?"

I thought about the years of sexless marriage . . .

"Hard to tell," I muttered.

"They say the wife is always the last," said Betty.

I sipped my drink.

"And Wendy's really upset," said Amy.

I choked. "Wendy?"

"Yes," said Amy.

"*Wendy* Wendy?" I said.

"Aye, that Wendy," said Amy.

"You mean *he's* gay?" I said.

"Everyone knew *he* was gay," muttered Danny. "I mean, look at the cottages—they've more cushions than a show home."

I didn't, I thought.

"He's only married to *her* to keep his dad happy," said Danny.

"But all those women," said Betty.

I blushed.

"He always liked to watch rugby," muttered Steven. "Now I know why."

"Put it about like a prize bull," said Betty.

I blushed bright red.

"The women who cried on my shoulder," said Betty.

I fanned my face. "God, that fire's hot."

"No, I think he really likes rugby," said Amy.

Sheryl asked me if I was all right.

I felt weird . . .

He said the sex was great, I thought. *Better than great—mind-blowing. Come to think of it, there was an excessive amount of blow jobs . . .*

"I had no idea," I muttered.

"Neither did I" said Betty.

I was playing the drums in the garage below my flat with Danny. The sun was streaming through the open garage doors as a Hossam Ramzy CD was playing, and I was trying to follow with way too much force.

The Bag Lady had lent me her African drum, and I was thrashing it like a toddler on saucepans. Danny was looking fresh, like he'd shaved and washed his face, and his hair, instead of sticking to his skull, flopped about his eyes.

I marvelled at the changed man.

How could a meeting over an automatic till have such an effect?

Sheryl, with her lusty laugh, told me it wasn't just the Bag Lady but *me.*

According to her, teaching me gave Danny "something to stay sober for."

I had my doubts . . .

I mean, it's not easy following along with a genius.

"Chill out," shouted Danny, running his fingers through his hair—his usual response when I cocked up a rhythm.

We had plans to play for Neff's belly dancing class when it got off the ground, which was just an excuse to explore Danny's favourite drum, the Egyptian tabla.

I'd first heard the tabla when I was outside Sheryl's new home. The night was clear, and it was a full moon.

Amy and I had spent the day looking at wedding dresses for her, and I ended up completely losing it with a parking attendant. I was feeling pretty bad, ashamed of myself; it seemed that every time Amy mentioned her father, anger consumed me, turning me into a mental woman who belonged in a straitjacket.

No wonder she didn't want to be seen with me.

I arrived at Sheryl's home, my stomach churning with emotion. I was like Basil Faulty in *Faulty Towers*, looking for something to smash, until I heard the tabla, and each beat touched me inside. It was so familiar, like from a past life. I stood for ages outside the house staring at the stars, the rhythm quenching my anger, until the laughing and the clapping overpowered the music . . .

I never thought any more of it until Amy's wedding, when I met Danny. He was half cut at the time, talking about his travels and all the different drums he had tried.

"The tabla," he said, "gets you right here." He gestured to his groin.

When I didn't react, he played.

Dum tak, dum dum tak . . .

Danny had lived many lives in many places, and he returned home with an earthy sense of humour and no one to share it with.

"I used to drink with my pals," he said. "Now I drink alone."

I wanted him to teach me. I wanted to feel what I felt outside Sheryl's house again and told him I would "start with anything."

Danny's eyes lit up.

The first lesson was me watching Danny zone out on a basic Masmoudi rhythm, his hands casually flicking across the top of a tabla. His moves were as natural as breathing, and I was back looking at the stars . . . at peace.

It's like great sex . . .

Of course, meeting the Bag Lady took Danny's drumming to a completely new level. He embraced her campfire like he had come home and spent the night "owning" the drum, with the Bag Lady memorised, like she had met her drumming god.

Her best friend Betty hadn't a clue.

She tried to join in with a tambourine, which was swiftly removed; an old pair of castanets from the second-hand shop, which landed in the fire; and two sticks, care of Danny, which followed the castanets.

The Bag Lady had no time for Betty's lack of rhythm.

Chapter Twenty-One

THE NEW JOB

The sign of a great sex life is the increased amount of sheet-changing.

The garage was *the* place to learn the drums: with the doors open, you had a view of the garden and an audience of one: Puss in her sphinx pose.

I didn't see Sheryl slip in the side door with Amy until she killed the music and started shouting about Beatrice complaining about the noise.

I carried on . . .

"She wants to know if you'll still be playing when she gets back," shouted Sheryl.

I thrashed a few beats . . .

"Cause if you are . . ." yelled Sheryl.

I stopped.

"She's getting earplugs," muttered Amy.

"Was I loud?" I said.

"Loud?" said Amy. "They can hear you in the co-op." Amy eyed my red sweaty face. "Have you been at the whisky?"

"Who needs whisky when you can take things out on a drum?" I said, tapping a few beats. I stopped. "I suppose we could use a break."

Danny didn't argue.

I poured him tea, slid in a spoonful of sugar, stirred, and handed it to him.

He stirred several more sugars into his tea, sipped, then paused with an "arrrrgh." "I'm heading off to Neff's after this," he said. "For dinner—mash and gravy." He licked his lips. "Beats pot noodles."

"Mash by the fire?" I said.

"Nah, inside. Neff's cooking."

"She's cooking?" said Sheryl.

"Yes, she says she's an expert in all things that grow under the ground," said Danny.

"Pfff," said Sheryl.

"And the Bag Lady has a cold." He smiled with a few playful taps on his drum. "I'm to bring some whisky and a rub for her chest."

"A rub for her chest?" said Sheryl. "What do you know about chest rubs?"

"Enough to buy a jar of Vicks VapoRub at the chemist." He sniffed.

Amy had that look again—a look that had me troubled, knotting my stomach. All this Richie stuff so soon after the wedding had me feeling bad about myself, and Amy talking about Henry sorting the kitchen didn't help.

Richie was moving in.

I told myself *not to give a shit,* that Richie and Henry had nothing to do with me, and I nearly kicked myself when I started asking questions. It was like my stupid mouth had a life of its own . . .

"What about the hotel and things?" I said, attempting a "Danny" flick on my drum. It sounded like I'd kicked a tin can. "I thought Richie ran the inn."

"Wendy's taking care of the inn. She and Richie's father are like *that* . . ." Amy crossed her fingers.

"Pfff," said Sheryl.

". . . and Richie's happy, relieved about the whole thing," said Amy, "so Dad reckons."

"That Wendy treated me like I was invisible," snapped Danny. "I was over there playing drums with the band, and all we got was a mug of lukewarm tea and a few digestives. You could have washed your face in that tea it was so weak. No sandwiches or free drinks; that woman is as tight as this here drum skin. At least the ex tossed a few crisp packets our way when we played."

Sheryl began to talk about the kitchen, the grubby behind of the Ferry Inn. "That place is as run-down as Beatrice's ex–Red Cross wheelchair," she said, and when she moved on about how the staff moaned, my mouth just butted in like it had a life of its own.

"So what was all that winking about then?" I said to Sheryl.

Shit . . . stop asking, I told myself.

"Winking? He was winking?" said Sheryl.

"Yes, at me," I snapped.

Shut up, I berated myself.

"Henry?" said Sheryl. "Was winking at you?"

"No, Richie," I said, almost kicking myself. *Cut it out with the questions.*

"Nervous tic, all the toffs have 'em," said Danny.

"Richie's hardly a toff," muttered Amy.

"He was definitely winking," I said. "I know a friggin' wink when I see one." I was really annoying myself now.

"All right, keep your shirt on," snapped Danny.

"That Richie gives me the shivers," said Amy.

"Thought you liked him," said Sheryl.

"When I was a kid," said Amy.

"I thought he was your best friend . . . thought he was everyone's best friend," I muttered.

"Hardly—he's had the sex life of a prize bull in a good old-fashioned farm," said Danny. "Lot of disappointed men and women out there."

I was starting to feel uncomfortable.

"I was staying at a pal's place," said Amy. "We were outside . . . and there he was by a tree, with my pal's father . . ."

"Typical," snapped Danny.

"We all have secrets," said Sheryl. "Things we don't want to think about, rather forget."

"He's the last thing Dad needs," said Amy. "Dad's fragile at the moment after all that wedding carry-on; I mean, being the laughing stock of your local is not easy."

I thought about Janice and Janet. *He was hardly living it quiet. Jesus, maybe he had told them? My sex life would be all over Argyll if they knew.*

"Let's talk about something else," I muttered.

Sheryl patted me on the shoulder and whispered, "You're better off without him."

I jumped. *Does she know about me and Richie?*

"Henry's an arsehole," said Sheryl. She looked at Amy. "Sorry, but he is. They've been sneaking around for months—like no one knew."

"Sneaking around?" Amy looked at me. "I didn't know that."

Neither did I, I thought, but then I remembered Henry's reaction when I told him about Richie. I thought he'd punch Richie, give him a black eye. In fact, I was scared of what he would do. In the end, he didn't do anything to Richie, come to think of it. It was not that long before they were friends again . . .

"Does it matter?" said Danny.

"Wendy's my first client in the area," said Amy, "and what does Dad do? Hook up with her man. First he ruins my wedding, done up like some has-been strippergram, and now he's gay? And I thought the worst thing possible was watching my mum attack a parking attendant."

"Wouldn't be the first," muttered the Bag Lady.

"Sometimes I wish I never moved here," muttered Amy.

Chapter Twenty-Two

A GAY BONFIRE

Sometimes the best thing a woman can do is learn to change a tyre.

Richie didn't appear until after New Year.

He brought a pissed Henry home and helped him to bed . . . our hands touched, and I, it seemed, had nothing to lose.

It wasn't long before the vibrator was tossed in the back of the wardrobe alongside my redundant comfortable underwear.

The car became a shagging shelter, lying easier, and each time, I could not believe I got away with it and lied to myself, *never again—as if.*

Once I saw Richie's face, his wicked smile, I was a goner.

Richie was so delicious he seemed impossible to resist, and despite still hanging about with Henry, he told me our sex was the best, sometimes when Henry was in the other room.

Maybe he'd toss Wendy aside and marry me, I told myself. *They aren't happy—she's only in it for the money.*

I backed the wrong horse.

As the wedding approached, our sex became more adventurous, Richie more distant and as elusive as Scarlet Pimpernel, and our meetings on and off like a pair of knickers, tugging at my heart strings. One minute he was cold and the next warm.

Then, when he arranged for Wendy to buy me a birthday present, I realised we were on a downward slope.

She appeared with a garden gnome in a co-op bag. The same garden gnome that was to end its life decapitated in the neighbour's yard.

I didn't know what to say.

"This is more you than me," she said.

I stared at the round pot belly, wondering what she meant. *How could a garden gnome be anyone's thing?*

Apparently, it was an engagement present from a distant aunt of Wendy's known for her bad taste and love of all things tacky and red.

Suddenly, all those blow jobs I'd given Richie left a bad taste in my mouth.

He didn't care at all.

When Richie and Wendy tied the knot, I felt nothing; I was like a zombie watching a film. I stared at Richie's back as he waited by the alter, as Wendy walked up the aisle—all those moments . . . tenderness, kindness, and laughing.

I had read into it what I wanted and backed that wrong *fucking* horse.

I was drunk before I got to the wedding, didn't finish my meal, staggered home, and howled like a baby watching her mum disappear as the other guests at the wedding danced.

I suspected Henry knew, because he'd started to mumble things when pissed, but it wasn't until after Richie's wedding that he went in for the kill.

"You tell me who you've slept with and I'll tell who I've"—he belched—"done *it* with."

We both had had more than a few drinks, but still I was shocked when Henry told me about his special women friends and how they made it impossible for him to say no.

I, like an idiot, followed his confession . . . my shame laid bare for Henry to spit at.

At first, Henry was quite kind. "I am only telling you about my shags so you don't feel guilty," he said. "We are adults, after all."

Which he followed by not acting like an adult. He didn't talk for days, then he went ballistic. He smashed so many of my plants I gave up gardening. Amy came home and thought there had been a hurricane.

I felt nothing.

I remember driving past Richie's house and seeing his smalls hanging on the line alongside Wendy's. I felt like a single sock, worthless, who didn't deserve a pot plant let alone a garden.

My guilt followed me everywhere, and Henry, who never forgave anyone anything, didn't speak to me for months.

I spent years in silence, in a barren desert. I stopped drinking and didn't go out for a long time, until Amy left for Glasgow University and a burst tyre changed me for the better.

I stared into the bonfire, listening to the Bag Lady and Danny talking drum talk. Danny was doing his best to impress the Bag Lady and she was doing her best to remain detached.

It was a superb bonfire with fantastic drums, and here I was wasting my time racking up all that past Richie bollocks. It was years ago, another lifetime . . . but I had bumped into Richie a few days ago . . . and the memories and feelings had come flooding back like yesterday's indigestion.

It was one of those "fuck you" moments that hit you when you least expected it. A moment you weren't aware of until hours later, staring into a bonfire . . . with a bundle of notes in the breast pocket of your overalls, basking in the warmth of friends.

Sheryl and I were fixing a leak in Richie's family's Inn—Ferry Inn.

It was a place with prices that only a certain type of holidaymaker could afford, the sort who used the marina next door.

I, in baggy overalls and a tool belt slung about my waist, was giving Monty, Richie's father, an explanation about why a leak that had plagued the hotel for years was easier to sort than a flat-pack from IKEA.

Sheryl was by my side; she had no idea about Richie or that I had ever been to IKEA. She threw me a "your call" look and continued packing up, happy for me and my moment of DIY glory.

To be honest, I was a bit of an arsehole, mainly because Monty was bit of a prick. It was the whole women-in-overalls thing. He seemed to think we were a couple of lesbians with a point to prove and refused to believe that Sheryl, married with a child, had not been artificially inseminated.

Not all lesbians wear overalls, I wanted to shout. Instead, I bumped up the price.

Monty took one look at the bill and pulled out his chequebook as Richie appeared by his side, tubbier, greyer, and much more ordinary than I remembered.

"I had no idea that you two were lesbians," muttered Monty.

"Dad, not all lesbians wear overalls," said Richie.

I ignored his wink.

"Would it have made a difference?" I said.

Monty's pen, poised over his cheque, stopped.

"Let's just say I'm glad I didn't know," he muttered.

Richie's eyes crinkled into that delicious smile, and I automatically smiled my customer smile, unaware of it being a "fuck you" moment until I jumped in the van.

I was too busy thinking about the outrageous price I had just asked for, Sheryl's "really" look, and Monty not even faltering. He went from an arsehole to a decent ol' boy in the time it took for him to sign *Monique McArthur* on his cheque.

"We've had that leak for years," said Richie. "Even Henry couldn't fix it."

"My point exactly," said his father. "You saved us a fortune, that leak was ruining the kitchen." Monty smiled at me again and made to slip a few notes into my breast pocket.

I grab his hand with a firm man-to-man handshake, and accepted the tip as we deserved it . . .

Three twenties and a tenner, I thought. *Impressive.*

"Henry says we need a new kitchen." Richie laughed.

"You do," I said.

"Well, you're on speed dial," said Monty. "Any problems and I'm calling you two."

"Don't make it too long," I said, "that grill is as ancient as your chequebook. You need a new one, and a proper fan."

Monty nodded like he was deaf, like he had no intention on splashing out for a new one. He probably hadn't been in the kitchen for years.

"Seriously," said Sheryl, "for your own safety."

"Aye, very good," he nodded, slipping our card into his breast pocket.

Sheryl and I split the tip.

I bought a drum and she a "come get me" bra, putting the sort of smile on Steven's face I hadn't seen since Baby Bea had been born.

Chapter Twenty-Three

MARILYN MONROE

One person's birthmark is another's eyesore.

When Beatrice came home that night, she was in a bit of a pickle.

George had left her in the kitchen, and she had tried to make herself toasted cheese and ended up on the floor.

I don't know how making toasted cheese led to her being sprawled out on the floor like a starfish, but there she was under her kitchen table, staring up at a century of cobwebs.

I was locking up the garage at the time, pondering toasted cheese myself, until I remembered I was a vegan.

I was thinking about Amy "doing Wendy's books," and to be honest, I felt a little sick. I had no idea what Wendy knew about Richie and me. She stopped speaking to me soon after the wedding, but I was worried . . .

What if she knew something? Would she tell, spill the beans?

I heard a crash from Beatrice's kitchen window, followed by a "fuck's sake" and a "friggin' hell."

Puss, who was parading about the cat flap, jumped.

Then my phone went . . . it was Beatrice with a snappy cry for help.

I walked into Beatrice's kitchen to see Beatrice's wheelchair upside down blocking the doorway, the fridge open and on its side, the floor covered in tomatoes in various stages of mush, one lonely chilli, two bananas—one oozing from a split in its skin—a tub of Betty's best massage oil, and Beatrice's outstretched hand clutching her mobile.

Puss sniffed the banana and jumped like it bit back.

"You took your time," snapped Beatrice.

Without a word, I moved her wheelchair.

"I mean I could have been dying here," she snapped.

I said nothing. I was too busy taking in the chaos and the naked legs of Beatrice splayed before me like porcelain treasures. I had never seen her legs before; they were much longer than I expected and, despite being of "not much use," were quite beautiful.

Denying any pain, Beatrice refused help.

"No medical idiots or Sheryl," she said. "I don't want neighbours knowing my business." *Despite the fact that we live up a lane and out of sight.*

Truth was, she was in the sort of outfit that didn't cover much, despite a decent-sized kitchen table covering her.

I poked my head under the table. "Where's George?"

Puss pawed the banana.

"He's gone for the codpiece . . . I mean, cod and chips." She glared at me, daring me to smirk.

"I see," I muttered.

"I was fed up waiting, decided to make something to eat, but some friggin' Bozo-the-Clown put the toaster in the most stupid place you could imagine—above the friggin' fridge."

Puss pounced on the banana; it oozed across the floor.

I lifted the massage oil with a questioning look.

"Collateral damage," she sniffed. "Just put it somewhere, out of sight . . ."

Puss skidded on the banana, then turned to see if anyone saw as I surveyed the tub of oil. I sniffed it, waiting for a Beatrice explosion.

"Look," snapped Beatrice. "Will you just help me? I don't want George walking in and spoiling our moment."

"I think the moment has been and gone," I muttered, and I was about to suggest calling George when Beatrice stopped me . . .

"Did you hear something?" she hissed.

"No." I looked about.

"That?" she whispered.

"What?" I said.

"Shhh—did you lock the door?" she whispered again.

"Why would I lock the door?" I said.

"Cooee!" came the voice of Ms Frasier.

"Bollocks," hissed Beatrice.

"Anyone there?" yelled Ms Frasier.

"Bugger and shit!" hissed Beatrice.

We heard the front door open . . . footsteps, two at a time.

"She mustn't find me," hissed Beatrice. "Quick, hide."

"What? Where? How?" I said, stupidly wondering about a tablecloth.

"Beatrice?" yelled Ms Frasier.

We heard a knock . . .

"I just came around to see . . ." The kitchen door burst open. "Jesus!" said Ms Frasier.

"Yes, all right, it's not as bad as it looks," came Beatrice's muffled voice from under the table.

Ms Frasier looked from me to Beatrice's legs. "Looks like the ol' sixth sense is still working then."

"We are perfectly fine, Ms Frasier," said Beatrice. "Helen's got everything under control, no need for you to worry. If you could just let Puss out on your way home."

Puss, mid paw licking, looked up with a "Moi? Going out? Don't think so."

Ms Frasier surveyed the table like a mechanic examining a car crash. "I could feel it in my bones that there was something wrong. 'Beatrice needs you,' my stomach told me . . ." Ms Francis tutted. "Never fails."

"As I said," yelled Beatrice, "if you just take the cat on the way out . . ."

Ms Frasier poked her head under the table and surveyed it like a mechanic now under the boot of the car at said car crash. "'Hurry,' my sixth sense was telling me, 'don't wait till tomorrow.'"

"Thank you for your concern, Ms Frasier, but if you and your sixth sense could kindly see to Puss on your way out . . ."

Ms Frasier stood and looked up at me. "The first thing we need to do"—she gestured to the table—"is move this."

"You're not touching my fucking table," snapped Beatrice.

Ms Frasier, without a word, mimed a "you take that side."

"I said," snapped Beatrice, "you're not touching my fucking —table."

We lifted the table . . .

"Oh, bugger," mumbled Beatrice.

Ms Frasier and I stared down at Beatrice, who was trying to retain her dignity with a blonde Marilyn Monroe wig, askew red lips, a pencilled-in birthmark, and a baby-doll knit dress with matching G-string, exposing a recent visit by Beautician Betty, who not only claims to "wax with no pain" but also to "get into the nooks and crannies others miss."

Without a word or a look at any nooks or crannies, Ms Frasier nodded to the hallway as Puss jumped onto Beatrice's chest and began to purr.

Beatrice reached out to pat. "There there, Puss . . ." she muttered.

Ms Frasier swiftly righted the table as I found a towel to cover Beatrice. She straightened it about her pelvis and muttered, "George will be back soon."

"Yes, and when he arrives, he'll find you ready for action," said Ms Francis, sliding the massage oil into a drawer.

A couple of hours later, the three of us were sitting around the table with a bottle of whisky, a box of vegan chocolates, and plate of toasted cheese, bubbling and hot. Beatrice, minus her wig, lipstick, and birthmark, was looking comfortable in her watching-TV pj's, while Ms Frasier, flushed from whisky, was looking like she had sorted the world.

It hadn't taken long to right Beatrice; she was light and easy to help, and soon she was staring at her bedroom mirror, lipstick poised, when George texted.

"He says he's held up at Steven's," I said, handing Beatrice her phone.

She waved it away.

"That's the mood fucked then," she said with a casual toss of her lipstick, followed by her wig. She looked relieved . . .

"He'll be ages," Beatrice shouted to Ms Frasier.

Ms Frasier didn't answer.

She was bustling in the kitchen, sorting things with a great amount of chair-scraping, cupboard-slamming, and hoovering.

Once Beatrice was deposited in her bedroom, Ms Frasier, shutting the kitchen to Puss, began cleaning in silent army emergency mode. She cleared the tomatoes, saving any good ones, straightened the table and the fridge, rearranged chairs, organised cupboards, mopped and hoovered for what seemed an eternity, and was just in the process of putting the toaster within wheelchair's reach when Beatrice crashed open the door with hers, covered up and confused.

Ms Frasier had been silent for way too long.

Beatrice looked about her pristine kitchen, then, after several cupboard searchings, pulled out a whisky bottle.

Ms Frasier poured while I fed Puss and found the chocolates.

It took several minutes for the whisky to hit and the silence to break.

Chapter Twenty-Four

DIY

A codpiece in the hand is worth two in the bush.

It was Beatrice who started . . .

"Sometimes you feel you should be doing something when really you'd rather not," she said, sliding a caramel between her lips.

Puss landed on her lap and Beatrice, without looking, stroked.

Puss purred.

"At our age, there are no *should-dos*," said Ms Frasier. "I mean if you can't do what you want at our age, then what is the point of all these friggin' wrinkles?"

Beatrice laughed; I said nothing.

"Never did like Marilyn Monroe," said Ms Frasier.

"Oh?" said Beatrice. "How's that?"

I kicked her under the table with a "don't get her started" look, then realised Beatrice wouldn't feel it.

"Too much like my mother. Most women were baking cakes and cleaning windows; not my mother. She hung about hotels. Lost count of the fathers I've had, the nameless men she enjoyed. She stopped doing what she should do way too young, when I was still riding second-hand bikes and reading cast-off *Dandy* comics."

Ms Frasier stopped, sipped her drink.

"She modelled herself on Marilyn Monroe, said fantastic kissing was good for the soul."

"Yes, well . . ." muttered Beatrice.

"She was an idiot," jumped in Ms Frasier. "Why would a ten-year-old want to know about kissing? She spent more on underpants than food. When she died, there were drawers of 'em. I could have carpeted Buckingham Palace with 'em twice over!"

Ms Frasier topped up her glass.

"You knew about your mum's men friends?" I said.

"I mean honestly," said Ms Fraser. "Who looks at knickers when you're shagging? If it's good, they're off quicker than a hiccup."

"Well, that's not strictly true," said Beatrice.

"I saw more men in my childhood than in the army," said Ms Frasier.

"Did you know what they were up to?" I said.

"Up to? My granddad used to come around and shout, called her all sorts of names. He didn't leave much to the imagination, he was like a sergeant major. Poor Mum didn't stand a chance—he bossed, bribed, and humiliated her."

"Well that's all well and good," muttered Beatrice, "but—"

"My mother used to put me in other people's clothes. She wanted me to be a mini Marilyn Monroe, pretty like her. I used to feel like an alien, like I was wearing someone else's jockstrap."

Beatrice looked at me and laughed. "And I bet you hated her," said Beatrice.

"Well, no . . . yes . . . I mean, sometimes." Ms Frasier looked at me. "Every daughter hates her mother sometimes."

"Not every daughter," I said.

"Not my Sheryl," muttered Beatrice. "She's kind, like her Gran."

"Most of us are like our grans. That's what the Aborigines say, although they don't call 'em *grannies*. They have a saying—"

"Aye well, most folk have sayings," said Beatrice.

"But Aboriginal sayings are different," said Ms Frasier. "When I was in Australia . . ."

Beatrice looked at her watch and began to mutter about George.

All three of us were pretty pissed by the time George arrived. It took one large whisky for George to catch up and another to turn him into a blether as prolific as Ms Frasier, who was seriously making me feel paranoid. Her talks of her mother and what she "got up to" had me squirming uncomfortably, and I wondered how much my Amy knew of my past—and if she did, did she judge, hate, or understand?

Beatrice looked at her partner. "No fish and chips then?"

"What?" said George.

"I said no *cod* and chips?" She nodded to Ms Frasier and me.

"Cod and . . . oh yes, *well,* I got held up at Steven's. It was all a bit" —he looked at me —"dramatic."

I slid the toasted cheese towards George. "Here, keep your strength up."

"Probably won't need it now," he muttered with a glance at Beatrice.

George had spent the evening at Sheryl and Steven's, listening to both moan about Wendy and her "imaginary complaints." According to George, Wendy had given Sheryl "a hard time" about our recent work in the Ferry Inn, claiming that our "DIY efforts" had brought on "a bigger, no, make that massive, leak."

"How dare she call you DIY," said Beatrice.

"She's really come into her own, surprised everyone," said George. "Apparently she's quite bolshie."

"Sounds like it," muttered Beatrice.

"I know her sort," said Ms Frasier. "She's the getting-even sort, the I-never-forget sort."

I tutted . . .

Wendy appeared all fragile and needy, milking sympathy, but underneath she was as ruthless as a starving lion. She was the sort that always had a problem, someone to blame, and an army of listeners. "She could make Santa Claus appear a complete bastard," I muttered.

No one heard.

The three of them had moved on as swiftly as a seagull dive. George was now on about his "notion" and how it had dissolved quicker than an Alka-Seltzer, and Beatrice and Ms Frasier, drinks poised, were on the edge of their seats.

"By the time I was on my third coffee," George said, "the idea of cod"—he glanced at Beatrice—"was as temping as last night's pizza."

Ms Frasier chuckled.

"The last time I saw Wendy," I said, "I was still married to Henry. We had just finished helping Amy move to college in Glasgow. Henry and I had a row over a flat tyre. She, of course, was on his side. He even gave her Amy's address so Wendy could 'keep in touch.'"

No one heard, but thanks to a decent amount of whisky, I didn't care and carried on.

"It was the day I changed my own tyre and realised if I could do that, then what was the point of Henry? Wendy, of course, came to his aid."

Still no one heard . . . George was topping up our glasses as Ms Frasier teased Beatrice and almost had her blushing.

"Cod?" said Ms Frasier, attempting a coquettish look.

"Aye, battered-like . . ." He looked at Beatrice. "And of course, chips."

"You and your cod and chips." Ms Frasier laughed.

"I don't know what you mean," said Beatrice.

I give up, I thought. *No one is listening.*

"Nothing goes by unnoticed here, you should know that," said Ms Frasier.

I shifted uncomfortably.

"The day *your* George walked into the Red Cross Store and bought Neff's codpiece was the day your sex life became a public affair. Everyone knew by the time he'd left the shop."

"My George?" muttered Beatrice.

"Neff and Rodger's codpiece had found a new home," said Ms Frasier.

"Don't be ridiculous," snapped Beatrice.

"It was around the WRI quicker than a stink bomb."

I looked at my phone. Sheryl had texted, asking if George had arrived.

"Arrived?" I texted. "They're all pissed, talking about bleeding cod and the like. I could rip my top off and no one would notice."

"Must you be so earthy?" Beatrice snapped at Ms Frasier. "And what's the WRI got to do with it?"

"And I for one am quite jealous," said Ms Frasier. "I mean a codpiece at your age is pretty impressive."

"My age? What's that supposed to mean?" snapped Beatrice.

"And in a wheelchair," said Ms Frasier.

"I still get about, you know," said Beatrice, "feel things."

"Exactly." Ms Frasier thumped the table. "You're an inspiration. As the Aborigines used to say—"

"Fuck the Aborigines," said Beatrice.

"Beatrice, you're very grumpy," said Ms Frasier with another rubbish coquettish look. "I think you're needing a good seeing to."

George choked on his whisky.

"Now they're talking about Aborigines—yet again," I texted to Sheryl. I waited for her usual LOL and a dozen smiley faces . . .

"The Aborigines have a saying," said Ms Frasier. "A witchetty grub in the hand is worth two in the bush."

George and Beatrice laughed, jolting Puss off Beatrice's knee.

George slid a chocolate between his lips and lifted Puss onto his lap.

While I, sober and speechless, read Sheryl's text . . .

"That Wendy is some cow. She's been putting it about how rubbish we are. Calling us D-fucking-IY and worse!!! She says we owe her and we either sort the leak for free, *as friggin' if,* or she's going to look elsewhere and send us the bill. Aye fucking right." Plus a frowny face way too many times to count.

Chapter Twenty-Five

DANNY

Life is like a cupcake: you need to eat the cake to truly enjoy the cherry.

Danny was around the next evening for our drum practice. He was setting up his drum and the music, while I was making coffee the way he liked it, extra strong with lots of milk and sugar. I was in full moaning flow about Wendy, and Danny, engrossed in his "setting up," looked like he wasn't listening.

He was flicking through his CDs. We were working our way through his Hossam Ramzy collection.

Danny had a good-old-fashioned CD player and a stack of good-old-fashioned Egyptian CDs. He had moved from LPs to tapes to CDs and was "not friggin' moving to any other so-called technology."

I watched him engrossed in his task . . .

"Did you hear me?" I said.

He continued to thumb through his CDs. "*Egypt Unveiled, Best of Saidi, Best of* . . . hmmm, there it is: *Rock the Tabla* . . ." He looked at me. "You up for something tricky?"

"She called us DIY," I said.

He tutted.

"I mean, me, DIY? Who the hell does she think she is?"

I slid another sugar into his coffee. He watched me stir with anger.

"That's not cement you're mixing," he said.

"The last thing I'm doing is giving her something for fucking free," I snapped, plopping another sugar into his mug.

"Easy on the sugar," he said.

"She's trying to ruin our reputation," I said.

I slapped the coffee in front of Danny and began to make mine.

He sipped . . . "A woman scorned and all that."

"What?" I said.

He slid the CD into the player. "You heard me."

I pretended to listen to the music; he looked at me.

"Is that me or her scorned?" I finally asked.

Danny looked at me.

"Everyone knows about you and Richie," he said. "It was Ms Frasier who told me."

I nearly dropped my coffee. *Ms Frasier?* I thought. *How the hell did she know?*

"It was Beatrice who told her," said Danny, scanning my face.

Beatrice? I thought. *Fucking hell—how did she know?*

"Sheryl told her," said Danny.

"Oh, God," I muttered.

"She said not to mention it, though, as you were still recovering from the wedding and were riddled with guilt. In fact, she wondered if perhaps the whole temper thing was because of your guilt."

Shit! I thought. *It was like being caught all over again.* I started to shake.

"She told me about the parking attendant too," he said.

He turned the music up.

I turned down the music . . .

"*She?* Who's *she?* And don't say the cat's mother . . . hate that."

"But who gives a shit about a parking attendant?" said Danny. "I mean anyone that puts one of those mongrels in their place is a star in my book."

He turned the music up.

I switched off the music.

"Who's *she?*" I said.

Danny turned the music back on.

"Play your drums," he said.

"Just tell me," I shouted over the music.

"Does it really matter?" he said.

He pushed the flat tar drum my way. I held it in my hand, trying to concentrate on the beat.

It wasn't working.

"If you must know," Danny shouted over the music, "it all started with Steven. He knew and wanted to help."

I began to bang way too hard. *So Steven knew as well,* I thought. *That pretty much included the whole fucking world . . .*

Focus on the music, I told myself. I could feel hot tears welling up. *Don't fucking cry . . .*

"Lost count of the married women I screwed," Danny shouted.

The song finished.

He laughed. "They were always willing, didn't put up a fight; do you see me riddled with guilt? Just wish the memory was better, some are a bit of a blur."

I wondered if Amy knew. *How could I find out? Should I just come out with it? Tell her her mother was a tramp, a slut who fooled around with her dad's new partner? Who had mastered the art of a blow job to the point that a gay man came back for more? Or hope, pray, cross my fingers that she didn't and never would find out?*

"There is nothing blurry about my memory." I banged the drum.

Danny turned the music off. "You underestimate folk. Many know how Henry treated you—no one worth a spit blames you, even Amy. She's a top girl. She says nice things about you."

I looked at him in disbelief. "After all the things I've done?"

"You're human, cut yourself some slack," he said.

"Easy for you to say, you don't have a daughter. You don't know what it's like. Sometimes being human isn't enough, especially when your daughter hero-worships your arch-rival."

"The only arch-rival in your life is you," said Danny.

I thought about Wendy and her DIY bullshit and threw him an *I doubt it* look.

Danny switched off the CD player. "I had a daughter."

I stopped, put down the drum.

"She was like your Amy: bright, busy, doing okay for herself, although how the fuck she managed that with my genes . . ."

"How old is she?" I asked.

Danny face fell as he told me about a woman who'd be about Amy's age. "She found out about me when she was fifteen, took her five years to find me," he said.

He looked down at the drum. "She was sitting in the audience where I was playing and came up afterwards. I hadn't a clue until she laughed—just like her mother. That night, we talked, and all I could think of was all those years I had no idea while there she was, around the corner."

I asked Danny what she was like. He described a young woman with dreams, someone he liked, felt he wanted to get to know.

"Her mother was just a fling, a married woman I hardly remember even when my daughter . . ." He stopped, blew his nose. "Even when she showed me a photograph. I think she was wanting a romantic story. I told her there was none, just a few drinks and a few nights; to be honest, I can't remember much."

He drained his coffee and pushed his mug towards me. "She's the reason I started to drink. We had one night, just one fucking night."

I stopped . . .

"She died a few days later in a car accident. I didn't find out till I looked in the paper. I stood at the back of the funeral. The only way I knew who her Mum was is because she was at the front and looked like her daughter. I don't think anyone recognised me; if they did, they certainly didn't let on. One even thought I was the gravedigger."

"I'm sorry," I muttered. "What was her name?"

"Megan," he said. "She was a belly dancer."

For a while, we sat in silence. I didn't know what else to say; neither did he. Finally, he flicked through his CDs and found a few slow songs. We played in silence, then, as he left, he grabbed my hand. "Nothing is that bad until it's gone for good."

Chapter Twenty-Six

A GRILLING

"Fuck you" moments happen when you least expect them.

I drove into the Ferry Inn car park not quite sure what to do, but I had to do something.

Sheryl was angry. She had spent the day moaning about "*her* who runs the Ferry Inn," calling her a "piece of work."

Steven suggested talking to Monty, which seemed like a good idea, except he was away for at least a month, while Beatrice suggested contacting Richie, who told Sheryl that it had nothing to do with him. *Typical Richie reaction.*

Ms Frasier wasn't much help either.

"A woman scorned is bad enough," she said, "but losing to another penis could send a woman into oestrogen overdrive."

Even Beatrice didn't have an answer for that one, and when Ms Frasier moved on to the Aborigines and their take on oestrogen, I nearly lost the will to think. Ms Frasier's advice was as much help as a "used condom, an empty packet of crisps and "to quote Beatrice, "yesterday's parking coupon."

I had to do something, because I suspect it was partly—if not all—my fault, and calling Wendy a "tit" wasn't going to make things better.

I mean, Sheryl didn't deserve to be slagged off, and I was also worried about Amy . . . the Ferry Inn was her first client, and the last thing I wanted to do was be the reason for it all to fall through, give her another reason to hate me.

Wendy was in reception waiting. I could see her thin silhouette in the window as I pulled up.

I decided to visit after a day's work, when I was full of masculine confidence and still in my overalls. Overalls are not only comfortable, but they make me feel in control and powerful. You can really strut in overalls, not to mention squat, reach for things, or jump out of a car, and there is always room for tools . . .

I dropped Sheryl off at her home and, without letting on, headed for the Ferry Inn. I knew Wendy would be there; I had texted her.

"We've things to sort," I wrote.

"Any time after five," she texted back.

With my tool belt slung about my hips like a gun holster belt, I walked into the Ferry Inn. It was quiet, the corridor empty, apart from an abandoned Hoover; my work boots clomped on the carpet, my tool belt rattled. I felt like I was in a Western as each step echoed into the silence.

A cleaner peered from a doorway, quickly dragging the Hoover out of sight; a waiter appeared, saw me, and scuttled back into hiding.

She was waiting at reception.

As soon as I saw her, I realised there was no leak, just an angry woman with something to say. She eyed my overalls and suggested the janitor's room. I followed past the office I had shaken hands with Monty in and the kitchen where a portly chef was shouting at a thin cook, both who, with a glance at me, were silenced.

Wendy pushed open the door with her foot and, after several attempts, cleared the doorway and gestured me in.

She looked different from the Wendy who had visited Henry and I. She was leaner and much more self-assured, with long red luxurious hair, which she flicked like in a shampoo ad with her tiny hands—the sort of hands that had never seen a hammer.

She had aged annoyingly well.

"How's Amy?" she said, pushing a footstool my way for a seat.

"Okay. Looking forward to working with you," I said, still standing.

She smiled to herself, made to perch on the stool, then stood again. "And you?"

"You know why I've come," I said.

"Do I?" she said cryptically.

"Of course you do. I've come to sort all this bullshit leak business," I said. "I can't have you telling the world porkies, can I?"

"You've not come for someone's husband then?" she said.

Silence . . .

"Or to make up some outrageous bill?"

"That bill was not outrageous," I said. "We fixed the unfixable."

"Like marriages then?" said Wendy.

I blushed, then pulled myself together. "Just show me where this so-called leak is and let me see what I can do."

"There is no leak," said Wendy.

I stopped.

"I just made it up."

I asked her why.

"To get you here," she said.

I asked her what for, and she glared at me.

"You know what for."

There was a knock on the door.

"What?" Wendy snapped at the door.

"Err, there's a phone call," came a soft voice.

"Can you not take a message?" yelled Wendy.

"Okay, it's just that, well . . ." said the soft voice.

"Just take a message," snapped Wendy.

"Okay." The door creaked open, and the cleaner peered from behind the door. "Sorry, just need the mop and bucket. There's been a bit of an accident in the kitchen."

"Here, take it," said Wendy, thrusting the mop at her.

"Can I get the bucket too?" said the cleaner.

"For heaven's sake," said Wendy.

She opened the door, slung the bucket at the young red-faced woman, and slammed the door shut.

"Now, where was I? Yes, I remember: shaming you."

"That was a lifetime ago," I said.

"Maybe to you," said Wendy.

Knock-knock—the cleaner reappeared. "Err, Wendy, I'm needing the detergent as well."

"For fuck's sake—here," snapped Wendy.

"That's the air freshener," said the cleaner. "I need the bleach and some . . . err, detergent."

I handed the detergent and the bleach to the cleaner; she caught my eye and smiled a "cheers."

Wendy slammed the door shut. "He was mine and you tried to take him."

"You weren't married then," I said.

"We were engaged, and you were a friend."

"Friend?" I said. "Hardly—you spent more time with Amy and Henry than me."

"Yes, well, Amy was better company," muttered Wendy. She stopped. And then she launched into a sermon about how much she hated *me*. "You and Amy, snuggled up on the couch, going fishing together, holding hands. I was so jealous," she said.

I was about to interrupt, ask what all this had to do with a leak in the roof and exactly when she'd had a hankering for fishing, but she wouldn't let me; years of anger spewed forth in a monologue fit for a soap opera. *Just as well I was standing comfortably.*

I slid my finger into my tool belt and, with my best bored masculine stance, continued to listen.

"Richie thought you were fantastic, and now Monty thinks you're the best thing since Tupperware ice cube holders—Jesus." Wendy took a breath.

"But you have all this," I said, gesturing to the cubbyhole.

"Oh ha ha, very funny." Wendy glared at me. "Always with the wit, trying to be funny. You—you took advantage—tried to split us up."

"Split you up?" I said. "I watched you get married. I was the one who looked like a tit."

"Yes, but look at you now," said Wendy.

"What do you mean?" I said.

"You've pulled yourself together."

"What?" I said.

"You even look good in overalls, while I'm left looking like an idiot losing my man to a fucking penis. Here's me watching my weight, dying my hair, spent a fortune on these nails . . ."

I was about to say "You're hardly the first," when I caught a look in her eye. *Is she tearful?*

"And Amy," she said. "I'd give anything for a daughter like Amy . . ."

Her face dropped; she paused for a moment, and her jaw wobbled. "Can't have children. Maybe if I could . . ."

I was moved, silenced, at a loss for something to say, when the fire alarm started.

She looked at me. "Just toast, I suspect."

It continued . . . followed by yelling and smoke.

The door flew open. "Quick the kitchen," shouted the cleaner.

I knew where the kitchen was. I ran down the corridor, Wendy following behind.

Chapter Twenty-Seven

THE FIRE BRIGADE

There is always another bin lorry.

There is nothing like saving the day to win folk over. But when you save the day with someone who you weren't too keen on, who you just found out hated you, then saving the day is something to be not only remembered but savoured, especially when it's all on a security camera . . .

The first thing I saw as I charged into the kitchen was the stunned face of the thin cook heading for the back door. He looked like a startled chicken, his spiky hair erect like a cock's comb, his eyes glazed in fear as his skinny legs skidded across the floor. He was clutching a pan of flames a mile high and licking the ceiling, flames fanned by his running, expanding with each step.

"What the fuck are you doing?" shouted the portly chef, his podgy red face streaming with sweat.

The thin cook stopped mid panic, juggling the pan like it was hot coals. Then he tripped. The pan toppled to the ground and flames spilled onto the floor, catching the wooden frame of the sink and making its way to the infamous greasy deathtrap of a grill.

"Jesus," yelled the portly chef.

He grabbed the thin cook's collar and pulled him from the flames; within seconds, the grill was alight like a bonfire.

Wendy tossed a fire blanket my way.

I tossed it on the flames. "Here's another," she shouted, and it was the beginning of a beautiful two-woman *let's save the kitchen* team that had the staff by the door watching in awe . . .

I've always been one of those people who's good in a crisis, so I'm told, but I *did it* in overalls and a fair amount of sweat and grunting. Wendy, it seems, with her tiny hands and perfect hair, *did it* while keeping her model-like looks.

We worked like we could read each other's minds, quickly placing all three fire blankets in place. Then Wendy ripped open an extinguisher, tossed it to me like it was a Coke can, and, without breaking a nail, ripped open the other extinguisher.

We showered those flames like a young male teenager after way too many pints of lager, and just like that teenager, our aim was strong and far-reaching and went on for ages.

By the time the fire brigade had arrived, the grill was covered in fat fire foam, the thin cook was draining a glass of water, and Wendy and I were basking in a round of applause from the staff.

That fire didn't stand a friggin' chance.

"You just don't think, do you?" muttered the thin cook to himself with a philosophical shake of his head.

He looked like he should be back in school, like he was young enough to enjoy a Happy Meal at McDonald's. I wanted to pack him up and put him on the school bus.

I patted his limp shoulder.

"Don't worry, it takes a few crises to learn not to panic," I said.

"I mean you're told not to do what I did," he muttered, "everyone knows, and yet all I could think of was if *she*"—he gestured to Wendy —"sees this, I'm for the chop."

"Amidst all those flames, you were thinking about your job?" said Wendy.

"That'll be a first," snapped the portly chef.

"Well, yeah." He tutted. "I've a Toyota to pay for."

I looked at him. "You're old enough to drive?"

The young man didn't answer. He was still in shock, having been so close to a fire that the hair above his lips was singed.

The staff were told to leave and take Mr Toyota with them. "Take him to the bar, give him something sugary," said the chef, "since he was almost barbecued."

"Perhaps a vodka?" muttered the young man.

The kitchen was still thick with smoke, the tiles black and broken—some fused together, others on the ground, buckled and crumbled under the heat—and half hanging from the wall, buckled, teetering on a couple of loose screws, swung the way-out-of-date fan.

The firemen, large and interesting apart from the one tiny woman "fire-person," had invaded the small kitchen. They were walking about like extras out of *Backdraft*, completely at home.

"Aye, you'd be surprised what some folk do in a fire," muttered a fireman, aiming his axe at the grill.

His axe sliced through the blackened tiles; they crashed to the floor.

"This lot all needs to go," he said. "Fire hazard—could start again."

"All of it?" said Wendy.

"Better safe than sorry," he grunted with another crash of his axe.

The firewoman looked at us with a *typical* look.

"He loves to put on a show," she whispered to Wendy and me, "and you don't get much chance in this quiet town. Can't remember the last fire we've been to."

"Let's call it quits," I said to Wendy's back. "A truce?"

I was sitting at the bar in the Ferry Inn. The chef, the thin cook, the waiter, and the cleaner were sitting around the table by the empty fireplace, looking at their glasses drained of alcohol.

We could hear the firemen in the kitchen, crashing about and making things safe, and said little. Wendy had been generous with the booze, and the staff were looking at their glasses with an "I wonder if there's more" look.

The thin cook looked up at Wendy. She was standing behind the bar, my glass under the whisky optic.

"Double?" She turned to me. "You deserve it."

"How about me?" shouted the thin cook with a wave of his empty glass.

Wendy leaned over the bar, clutching her second vodka, and took a sip. "Need a lot of work from you once the insurance is sorted," she said.

"Work? A whole new kitchen's what you need," said the chef. "Been telling that father-in-law of yours for years, and that useless Richie—arsehole. If they'd listened to me, I'd still be in the kitchen deboning my chicken; fucking thing's cremated now." He lifted his empty glass and sniffed it. "Waste of a good hen."

She looked at me. "Richie can be a bit tight."

My mind flashed to the crappy gnome present.

"Tight?" said the chef. "Richie's idea of spending money on the kitchen was two bottles of bleach."

"From the pound shop," laughed the cleaner. "May as well try and clean with a cup of pot noodles."

The staff laughed, some with longing looks at their empty glasses.

"Aye, and our meals were leftovers," said the waiter. "Yesterday's unwanted."

"Well, that's not strictly true," muttered Wendy. "You could help yourself to the chips."

"How about we help ourselves to the bar?" said the thin cook.

"But," said Wendy, "there are gonna be a few changes around here." She began to fill the staff's glasses, then hurled a few packets of crisps at the staff's table. "No more of that crap for a start."

"Not that vegan bollocks again," sighed the chef. "I told you, cooking that stuff takes practise."

"You'll have plenty of time for that now," said Wendy.

A small chuckle rumbled through the staff as they began to rustle open the crisp packets.

Wendy turned to me. "I need to get hold of Amy. She can give me a hand with the insurance claim." She sipped her vodka. "She's a great girl."

"I know," I said.

"Give anything to have a daughter like her."

"So you said." I feigned a smile.

"She didn't bat an eyelid when she heard about you and Richie," said Wendy. "She's so loyal."

"What?" I said, my whisky poised. "She knows?

"Have another whisky," said Wendy with a sheepish look.

"Did *you* tell her?" I said.

"No," said Wendy, "merely confirmed like. Here, try a malt."

"I always thought it was Henry that would tell," I muttered.

"No, it was the postman," said Wendy.

I paused over a packet of plain crisps. "Must we talk about that here?" I gestured towards the staff, who'd hogged all the cheese-and-onion crisps.

"Pfff, they know everything," said Wendy. She downed her vodka. "Another?" She waved at the bar.

"Aye," came a chorus from the table.

"That postman's a fucking blether," said the chef through a mouthful of crisps. "Between him and the coal man, nothing's sacred; a dodgy shit wouldn't go past them."

The waitress slapped the chef's thigh with a "cut the swearing."

He glared at her and then at the thin cook, sniggering.

"She heard the postman talking to the coal man," said Wendy.

"He's good friends with the butcher," said the waitress, "who comes here with our meat."

"When we can fucking cook it," snapped the chef.

"I don't want to hear any more," I said.

Wendy topped up my whisky. "Does it really matter how she found out?"

"I didn't know you knew," I muttered, "let alone Amy."

"A partner always knows," said the cleaner.

"Well, I didn't know about Henry," I lied. *I did have suspicions . . .*

I slumped back in my chair. *What now?* I thought. *Would Amy hate me forever?*

"The point is, she's probably known for years," said the cleaner.

"She knew before she went to college," said Wendy with another sheepish look.

"Jesus," I said. "I don't know why we bothered to sneak around. Should have done it on the swing in the park, you could have all taken pictures. Catch the blow job that almost turned a gay man straight."

I turned to toast the staff, only to find the fireman known as "Boss" standing behind me.

I didn't know what to say. I stared at the kitchen crew sipping their free drinks. One raised a glass at me; the others followed.

Chapter Twenty-Eight

THE BOSS

Sometimes, calling it a day is as good as it gets for a happy ending.

I had no idea how long "Boss" had been standing there, but it was obviously long enough for him to be smirking like a sixteen-year-old surveying his first *Penthouse* magazine.

"We're almost done," he said to Wendy.

He patted her shoulder with a *fellow comrade* nod, *which I guess comes from looking like a model and saving the world.*

"If it wasn't for you, this whole place would have gone up," he said.

With a flick of her gorgeous red locks, she flashed a smile. "Yes, well, it's my job to save my business, but it's not hers," she said, gesturing to me. "Couldn't have done it without her. I mean there was no way I would have attempted anything if it wasn't for *her* jumping in."

Boss eyed me. "Always did like a woman in overalls."

A week later, Beatrice was in her kitchen trying to make me a hero's meal, despite not having any idea how to cook without bacon or chicken, let alone butter.

She was rummaging through the cupboards, cursing Ms Frasier's sorting, despite the fact that everything was at wheelchair level *and* labelled.

I watched her. When I first met Beatrice, I thought I'd met a real storm in a teacup, a melodramatic pain in the arse who made Sheryl's life as painful as a set of piles after a tandoori. Back then, I was so lonely that sometimes I'd put the satnav on and drive about in the car just to hear a voice.

Now, that storm in the teacup had turned out to be the sort of friend I'd dreamt of, although she still gave Sheryl a hard time.

After the fire, Beatrice brought in a pile of vegan chocolates, spent the week opening her favourite malt whiskies, and called me a hero several times.

No one had called me a hero before. My parents treated me like Beatrice treated Sheryl. Instead of calling me fat, they called me weak, and they never argued when Henry called me "Ms Nothing Special," "Whale Woman," or "Pissy Brecks."

Sometimes they even laughed.

Beatrice opened the kitchen window when I practised the drums; sometimes she even turned down her radio. My parents had no idea I played the drums, even though I sent them a picture.

It drove Sheryl mad. "What have you got that I haven't?" she said to me once, until her and Steven moved to their new home and started to look like they used to when they were first married. Then she didn't seem to care so much.

"Parents," she said. "You can't live with 'em and you can't live without 'em."

"That Ms Frasier really gets on my wick," said Beatrice. "I have my own system."

"Yes, what the hell was she playing at, helping you?" said George. "How dare she put everything in reach?"

George, after several offers to help had been met with "leave it" barks, had resorted to insults, which seemed to perk Beatrice up to no end. She bristled about the kitchen.

"How about an Indian," said George, "and one of Neff's quick-as-a-belch deliveries?"

Beatrice pulled a face.

"We could have curried vegetables here quicker than you could peel garlic," he said. "Once you've found it, that is."

Beatrice, with a "pfff," moved to another cupboard.

"Besides, the notion of a Beatrice meal is wearing thin," muttered George.

Beatrice let out another exaggerated "pfff."

"Chips and whatever is as close to my mind as yesterday's horoscope," said George.

"You never read the stars," said Beatrice. "And I never said anything about chips."

"My point," said George.

"Your point? You're way off the point. We'll be opening another whisky bottle if I have to listen to any more of your bollocks, then I won't remember anything you've told me."

"You don't have to drink it," laughed George.

"Oh ha ha," snapped Beatrice. She looked up from the under the sink. "Okay, then call that so-called belly dancer Sheryl and tell her to hurry up. Amy will be here any minute." She smiled at me. "Can't wait to see that delicious Baby Bea."

Beatrice closed the cupboard with a bang, pulling out another bottle of whisky. "Here we are, a malt for our hero," she said.

I hadn't been teetotal for days.

I stared out the window and caught Amy arriving. She was looking distracted, which by now I was getting used to.

Chapter Twenty-Nine

THE RISE AND FALL OF PUSS

There is not much choice of men after a certain age, you're never quite sure of the state of the underpants.

few hours later, Beatrice's garden table was covered in empty curry takeaway boxes, and we had all moved on to wine as Danny and the Bag Lady, who had come together, played their drums.

The sun had set, Sheryl had lit a fire, and we had all drunk enough to find Ms Frasier funny.

I thought about the past, for the first time without guilt. *I should be grateful,* I told myself. *If it wasn't for great sex, I may never have left a horrible marriage, believed in something better.*

Sheryl called me a hero, Danny "Saint Helen," while Amy almost looked impressed, but then she had had enough wine to have to stay at my place overnight. Still, I like to think that wine, like whisky, often speaks from the heart.

She had been at the Ferry Inn all day going through things with Wendy and the Boss fireman, costing the work needed to make a dilapidated kitchen into something worthy enough for vegan cordon bleu.

"That Wendy missed her calling," said Ms Frasier. "She should have been in the army . . ."

"Army, with those nails?" said George.

"The army bonds folk together," said Ms Frasier.

"Does it?" muttered George.

"Yes. When I was in Australia . . ."

Danny and the Bag Lady burst into a drum roll loud enough to drown out Ms Frasier and jolt Puss mid sniffing of a stray pakora. She raced up a tree and stared down at us like she had just seen a ghost pit bull.

Baby Bea did her best to coo Puss down and finally fell asleep on Beatrice's lap.

We all laughed our heads off and were still laughing hours later, until Puss began to dangle like Spider-Man; then, drunken panic set in.

Amy suggested calling "Boss" the fireman, as he lived just around the corner. "We're like that," she chuckled with crossed fingers.

"Let me be the hero!" I staggered.

Sheryl pulled me back. "Not in your state."

Apparently, "Boss," was delighted, and when he found out there was a selection of ladders to choose from, even more so. "Can't wait to see the infamous DIY Two's tools," he said, according to Amy.

"Will he be coming in his uniform?" laughed Ms Frasier, which everyone ignored.

We watched as he climbed the ladder, and Ms Frasier—who, according to her, had never seen a fireman—shouted, "Give me a cat, a decent set of teeth, and some lubricant, and I'm ready for anything."

"Perhaps you should go home," muttered Beatrice.

Puss, without a backward glance, hurled herself into Boss's arms and was purring before she hit his jumper. No one said anything, but everyone clapped furiously as Amy's distracted look finally melted into a smile.

Of course, Boss had to stay for a drink or three, and as there was no food left, Beatrice produced another tray of vegan chocolates and waved them under his nose.

"Vegan?" he said.

A few long faces nodded.

He looked at me. "I became a vegan the day I put out a fire at an Ann Summer shop."

I waited for him to explain, and when he didn't, I asked.

"I'll tell you tomorrow," he said. "After I've cooked you dinner."

I wouldn't say that Wendy and I became best friends or even "women who do Prosecco together." Within minutes of being in her company, I am bored, and she finds my sense of humour as funny as a "fanny fart" —which apparently she never does—but she gives us a lot of work.

She and Sheryl communicated well, so well that Wendy managed to whittle down our bill. She knew how to get around Sheryl's good nature and has her on speed dial.

And as for Richie and Henry, they remain together. Can you believe it? Both are a little fatter, often seen arguing over the cheese selection in the co-op; Richie still maintains that Dairylea cheese isn't real cheese, while Henry tries to sneak it into their basket when Richie is not looking.

The security camera film of Wendy and me is now used in fire safety training days; apparently, our use of fire blankets is a new technique taught during the day, and our spraying of the fire extinguisher gets a round of applause.

Wendy *had* told Amy about Richie and me; the whole "postman" story was an embellishment brought on by too much vodka and shock. But to be fair to Wendy, she couldn't have told Amy at a better time. Amy had seen the decapitation of the gnome from her bedroom window; she had seen her father in full bastard mode and found it easy to understand why I did what I did.

The closest Amy and I got to talking of the Richie days was the gnome. For some reason, one appeared in Beatrice's garden—a big fat red gnome.

Amy was the first to see it, jumping out of the van after a day's work in the Ferry Inn.

She stopped, brushed the dirt from its shoulder, and turned to me.

"Nice to see a gnome with its head attached," she said. Then she hugged me, and Amy's not really big on hugging.

****

Would you like to read more? Nefertiti's new passion, how Sheryl and Steven hit a dip, or even Ms Frasier's latest chaotic attempt at helping Beatrice.
Book 6 ***The Other Side Of Yes*** is on sale now
At your favourite store
Or if you want to try before you buy read on...

THE OTHER SIDE OF YES- CHAPTER ONE

Not every girl wants a doll

Sheryl

I was sitting in the garden watching Baby Bea play, while Mum relived the joy of seeing Mr Finlay's stiff socks.

Why she would remember I have no idea – she's never cleaned in her life. My Mum – Beatrice – has as much idea of cleaning for a living as the Pope has of a hen night. She doesn't even do her own laundry; she leaves it for me or her on/off partner, George. Apparently living in a wheelchair makes emptying a washing machine impossible.

Cleaning for the likes of Mr Finlay is a memory burned in *my* head, sorting through his smalls was best done with gloves, in poor lighting, while holding my breath. He had prunes with everything and liked to get the "most out of his underwear" with a sniff and throw test, which meant wearing his socks until they stood up on their own then tossing in the vague direction of the laundry basket. Mr Finlay's sense of smell was as buggered as my post pregnancy pelvis, you'd only have to open the fridge to testify to that and it was one of the few things Mum and I agreed on.

Mum and I had reached a turning point in our so-called relationship, a turning point lubricated by red wine and Baby Bea, my delicious daughter. Nagging is the furthest thing from my mother's mind when

Baby Bea is about. Her face lights up, sometimes she even laughs, with a "thank you for bringing her into the world" look at me.

It's enough to make me want to visit more.

We had just polished off a bottle of red and were waiting for Steven to pick Baby Bea and me up when Mr Finlay's hygiene became a discussion point.

Mum, her face a healthy sun and red wine flush, was dressing an old doll she had sourced from the Red Cross shop which Baby Bea had as much interest in as the six o'clock news. She was too fascinated by Puss, Mum's cat.

"That Mr Finlay had no shame," said Mum, see-sawing a bonnet for a golf ball size head onto a head the size of a football. "But then he was always a bit of a minger."

I stared at Mum. The last time she said minger, I was in short socks and wore a vest, Dad was still alive and the only reason she said it was to get his attention.

"Yes," she said, "a real minger, his smalls were as toxic as nuclear waste."

"Mum, the only smalls you've ever sorted is the change in your purse."

"Pity the poor ambulance man that finds him on the floor." Mum attempted a more prolonged stretch and hold motion with the bonnet. "They'll have to scrape him off with a spade."

"Mum!"

"What?"

"That bonnet is never going to fit on that head."

Baby Bea made a grab for Puss.

Puss escaped with a skid.

Mum tossed the doll, minus bonnet, across to Baby Bea.

The doll landed with a thud by her feet, its cotton-stuffed limbs spread out like a starfish.

Baby Bea burst into tears.

"That's Nefertiti's biggest fear," said Mum.

"You mean Neff," I said, moving towards my daughter.

Mum looked at me.

"What? She likes to be called Neff."

"First I've heard of it. I mean, it's hardly regal, is it?"

"That's what living in Lochgilphead does to you. No one gives a toss about that sort of thing here and who wants to have "Nefertiti" shouted out across the GP waiting room? In fact I think that's what made her give into the whole "just call me Neff" thing."

Mum sniffed.

"And when has she ever seen Mr Finlay's socks, anyway?"

Baby Bea picked up the doll and hurled it at Puss.

Puss made a dash for cover under a hydrangea bush.

"Not the socks," said Mum. "To be found by the ambulance man..."

"I see." But I was still confused.

"...Her body letting her down," Mum added, "in the sort of position even a porn star wouldn't want to be seen in. Especially with her underwear, well, not at its best."

I picked up Baby Bea and the doll.

Baby Bea pushed the doll away.

"But that's what the paramedics are there for," I said. "To deal with bodies letting you down. They've probably seen more minging underwear than I've seen dirty nappies."

"Don't say that word, Sheryl!"

"What?"

"It's a dreadful word."

"But you just said it..." I gave up, and plonked down beside her, Baby Bea in my lap.

Mum stretched out her arms and Baby Bea, doll forgotten, tumbled into her lap with a giggle. "Nefertiti...I mean, Neff, dreads the ambulance folk spreading soiled underwear rumours in the Co-op," she said.

"I wouldn't worry, those ambulance folk are sworn to secrecy," I said. "Confidentiality and all that. They'd have their tongues cut off and fed to the sausage factories if they said anything."

Mum threw me another "don't be ridiculous" look and then with an expert Baby Bea jiggle said, "Neff fears the bagging up of her things like yesterday's newspapers."

"I think you'll find it's the relatives who do that."

"Sent to the Red Cross shop for people like Ms Frasier to rummage through."

Mum always brought up Ms Frasier when exasperated, they had the sort of "love to prove each other wrong"' relationship which was worth watching as long as you didn't get involved. Ms Frasier had spent "her best years"' in the Outback and had a passion for second-hand shops or "Op shops' as she calls them. She's never out of the Red Cross Shop, pulling shirts and ties off the rack, reminiscing about the "poor dear departed, last seen only weeks ago, as fit as a Mallee bull". And no matter how many times she's asked what her first name is, Ms Frasier never replies. Mum recons she fancies herself as Lochgilphead's Columbo, while those in the Red Cross call her Inspector Morse – but behind her back.

"...and for once I agree," said Mum. "The last thing I want is my life reduced to underwear and false teeth shoved into a garbage bag."

'I thought you didn't care?" I said. "That you wanted to be cremated."

****

At your favourite store

The Real Story Of 'O'

First edition. 21st Feburary 2021.
Copyright © 2021 Kerrie Noor.
Written by Kerrie Noor.

❀ Formatted with Vellum